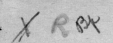

"What are you really like, Emily Becket?"
Noble asked, his voice barely a whisper.

His eyes asked the same question as he pulled her closer to him.

Emily felt her body responding to him and fought the urge to run away so he'd never know how he affected her. But she's almost stopped caring how big a fool she made of herself.

This was one night out of her whole life. One night when she could do anything she wanted to. Wear a plunging neckline. Look sexy and irresistible. Speak exactly what she thought. Melt for the most gorgeous man on earth and dance in his arms. What harm could one night of living in a dream do?

"I'm just like everyone else," she murmured. Only tonight she was a femme fatale, a man-killer.

"I don't believe you," Noble said.

Looking into his eyes, Emily felt herself drowning in a vat of hot fudge. "It's true," she told him. But she was ready to throw him to the ground and thoroughly ravish him. She shivered with the thought.

"Okay, be mysterious," he said. "I love uncovering secrets."

Then his eyes darkened with desire, his fiery gaze peeling back the first layers. . . .

WHAT ARE *LOVESWEPT* ROMANCES?

They are stories of true romance and touching emotion. We believe those two very important ingredients are constants in our highly sensual and very believable stories in the *LOVESWEPT* line. Our goal is to give you, the reader, stories of consistently high quality that may sometimes make you laugh, sometimes make you cry, but are always fresh and creative and contain many delightful surprises within their pages.

Most romance fans read an enormous number of books. Those they truly love, they keep. Others may be traded with friends and soon forgotten. We hope that each *LOVESWEPT* romance will be a treasure—a "keeper." We will always try to publish

LOVE STORIES YOU'LL NEVER FORGET
BY AUTHORS YOU'LL ALWAYS REMEMBER

The Editors

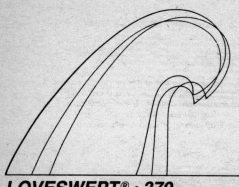

LOVESWEPT® • 370

Mary Kay McComas
Poor Emily

BANTAM BOOKS
NEW YORK • TORONTO • LONDON • SYDNEY • AUCKLAND

POOR EMILY

A Bantam Book / December 1989

ISBN 0-553-44007-1

Published simultaneously in the United States and Canada

Bantam Books are published by Bantam Books, a division
of Bantam Doubleday Dell Publishing Group, Inc. Its trade-
mark, consisting of the words "Bantam Books" and the
portrayal of a rooster, is Registered in U.S. Patent and
Trademark Office and in other countries. Marca Registrada.
Bantam Books, 666 Fifth Avenue, New York, New York 10103.

PRINTED IN THE UNITED STATES OF AMERICA

O   0 9 8 7 6 5 4 3 2 1

Katie
God blessed you with intelligence,
beauty, a sweet disposition and
a gentle heart. He blessed me,
with you. I love you.
Mom

Prologue

Spring 1863

"William Joseph, where you going? Your supper's ready."

"Be back soon," he told his wife as he picked up his rifle and walked to the door. The one-room cabin was thick with wood smoke, the odors of the pork back cooking in his wife's kettle, and overworked bodies. But that wasn't his reason for going outside, although there was no denying he'd welcome the fresh air. "Heard riders. If it's them damn Yanks comin' after more chickens or my water, they're gonna get more than they come for."

"Let 'em have what they want. One cripple can't fight the whole Union army. You got these children to raise," his wife reminded him plainly.

"I'll be takin' care," he said, opening the door with a loud squeak and hobbling into the night. He'd spoken with confidence, not so much to reassure the woman, but because he knew there was no danger awaiting him.

He'd been waiting and listening for this group of riders for over a fortnight now, and he was eager to join up with them again. If he hadn't taken the bullet in his leg nearly a year before, he'd be riding with them still. As it was, he had to meet comrades in the dark and smile at the enemy when the sun came up. It was nights like this one that made his smile come a little easier.

"William Joseph. That you?" a man called out in a hushed voice as he rounded the far side of the sty.

"Pitney? That you callin'." There was a rustling of leaves as four men emerged from the bushes and stepped into the moonlight. "Hell, man, why don't ya hide yourselves down by the chicken coops. Smells better," William Joseph admonished his friends as he pumped each of their hands vigorously, clapping their backs in welcome. "Better yet, if ya don't want the Yanks to smell ya, come on inside. Nobody comes within thirty miles of this place when the old woman's in there cookin'."

"Thought ya was gonna get yourself a new wife, William Joseph. A young one with yellow hair," John Finney said, laughing.

"Nah. I got this one all broke in, and my boys are fond of her. I may as well keep her till she dies," he replied easily, knowing his wife would skin him alive if she heard him talking about her in such a manner. Then again, everyone in the county knew his Maggie was a good ol' girl and that he wouldn't trade her for anything. "Tell me how you fared. Did all go as planned?"

"Like eating pot pie." Finney laughed. "We decked ourselves out in them pretty blue uniforms and met them on the road between Alexandria and the capital. Our source was good this time, right down to the last man. We rode in, put the gold in our bags, and hightailed it outta there. Them Yanks ain't gonna get new horses this winter," he said, shaking his head in mock regret. "It was almost too easy."

"A poor row, eh," he said, commiserating good-naturedly with his friend. Intuitively he knew there was more to the story than Finney was telling. But the basic fact that the deed had been done without mishap or casualties was all he'd really wanted to know. "Where's the lieutenant. I was hopin' to see him too."

"He's finishing up with Hanson. He had to round up a new chest to put the gold in. Told us to come ahead in case you'd heard us comin'. Didn't want ya to worry."

"No need to worry. Already told ya about the ol' lady's cookin'," said William Joseph, trying to make light of the fact that if the Union soldiers ever found out what he was doing, they'd very likely hang him and burn his farm to the ground.

"Becket." The voice came from behind the men. It was a voice they were all familiar with, a voice they followed without question, a voice filled with authority and confidence. It was the voice of Lieutenant Wakeland, their commanding officer—a man they feared and depended on at the same time.

"Sir," William Joseph said as he and the tall, lean Confederate officer shook hands and strained their eyes in the darkness to see each other's face. "Good to see you're well."

"Good to be so, Becket. We can't dally tonight. They're hot on our tails. If they catch us this far out, they're bound to know what we've done here tonight. You'll need to finish boarding it up, but we got it all in place with no trouble."

"Yes, sir."

"Thank you, Becket," Lieutenant Wakeland said as he took William Joseph by the arm and led him away from the others. Then in a lower voice he continued. "I know there's no need to tell you how important this is or what it'll cost you if anything goes wrong."

"No, sir."

"But just in case something does happen, I want your word that none of that shipment will ever fall into Union hands. If we don't come back for it, make sure it gets used for the good of the South."

"Yes, sir. You got my word on it."

The lieutenant seemed to relax. He took a deep, bracing breath of the cool Virginia night air and looked up at the stars. "They look so far away," he said as if thinking aloud.

"Yes, sir. Everything looks far away these days."

"That it does. It seems like a hundred years ago that I was just a simple schoolteacher whose greatest trial was trying to get children to do their sums."

"Didn't know you were a teacher, sir. I got a boy that can both read and write."

"Put him to good use, Becket. An education is worth more than a thousand of the shipments we stole tonight. If men were better educated, if they could learn tolerance through understanding, they wouldn't be chasing each other over the countryside trying to kill one another." He paused in regretful silence. "Enough of that. We must go. We'll walk out a ways and remount in the glen. The fewer people who know we've been here, the better off we'll be."

"I'm the only one, sir."

"Fine. Good luck to you, Becket."

"And to you, sir."

One

"Emily, you are a very strange person," Jennifer said, her expression emphasizing the remark.

"So you keep telling me." Emily was well aware of everything that even briefly crossed her cousin's mind. Jennifer hadn't the slightest compunction in speaking aloud her every thought.

"Well, don't you think it a little strange that when given a choice of birthday gifts, someone would choose wallpaper?"

"Not if that's what this someone wanted," Emily said mildly, studying a book of wallpaper samples the way Jennifer would a jeweler's showcase. "What do you think of this one?" she asked, more to herself than to Jennifer.

Her cousin glanced at the sample, rolled her eyes, then slammed the book closed with a heavy, dramatic sigh. "How about a new coat? That would be a very practical gift, and it would get this eyesore you're wearing off the streets at the same time. I swear, Emily, I'm almost embarrassed to be seen with you."

"Almost embarrassed?" Emily asked, taking no

offense. It wasn't just the coat Jennifer was objecting to. She'd been "almost embarrassed" by nearly everything Emily did, said, or wore for as long as she could remember. Every time they got together they had the same conversation. Jennifer would lead off with a disparaging remark and eventually would wind up asking why Emily had chosen to come back to Remount instead of keeping her job in D.C.

Emily's response was always the same, but just to give her cousin the impression that she *had* been giving her life some consideration, she would look thoughtful for a moment and then take a wild stab at the right answer. "I'm happy here?"

"You can't be."

"Why not?"

"Because that old barn of a house you live in is a disgrace—"

"It's a historical landmark," Emily injected calmly.

"You have no money."

"I have few needs."

"Your job is depressing."

"It's challenging and very rewarding."

"You have no social life in this dead-end town."

"I have many good friends," Emily said, and then added, "And I have you."

"Well, you're lucky to have me anyway," she'd say, shaking her head and giving her that poor Emily look. It was an expression Emily was very familiar with but one she'd never been quite able to understand.

There was nothing poor about Emily. To her way of thinking, she was one of the wealthiest women she knew. Not monetarily, of course, but in other ways. Ways that couldn't be measured.

Not that her life was perfect. Emily had her

trials and tribulations, just like everyone else. While growing up she'd wanted a sister—or a dog. She'd gotten neither. But she'd had loving, supportive parents and a pretty terrific childhood nonetheless.

After college she'd spent six years in the hustle and bustle of Washington, D.C., working with the Department of Health and Human Services and sowing herself a few wild oats. She'd returned to her childhood home after her parents had passed away, with a solid conviction that she was better suited to living the life of a medium-size fish in a small pond than the life of a guppy in an ocean.

There'd been minor disappointments, like learning to live with her curly brown hair, which came into fashion only every fifteen years or so; knowing that her mustard-brown eyes were too large for her face; and having to remember to suck in her bottom lip so she wouldn't appear to be pouty. She also thought it was taking Mr. Right an extraordinarily long time to show up in her life, but she figured these things were all pretty much fate-related and uncontrollable, so there wasn't much sense in worrying about them.

Rather, Emily liked to think that she was a healthy, intelligent, and capable woman who didn't have to perm her hair when curly was cool, that there was a chance she might meet the man of her dreams around the next corner, and that her life, in general, wasn't so bad.

"I'd be completely embarrassed if we were in Richmond," her cousin was saying. "But here in Remount, everyone knows you're a little off, that you've been this way since childhood—and that it has no reflection on me. What are you staring at?"

"Shh," Emily hissed, waving her cousin to be silent. "There he is. Across the street. Jogging.

See him?" Jennifer wasn't able to resist looking when Emily actually sighed in ecstasy. "Isn't he the most beautiful man you've ever seen?"

Jennifer narrowed her nearsighted eyes and gave this description careful consideration.

Emily, with her breath caught in her throat and her heartbeat skipping erratically, also gave careful consideration to the subject in question. She watched wistfully as the jogger ran past Trudy's Antique Shop on the other side of Main Street. He was tall and lean and graceful. His hair was dark and on the long side. She'd often wondered what color his eyes were, but she'd never seen him up close, only from a distance.

Some days he wore a sweat suit, but most days he wore shorts and a short tank top. She loved the way he held his arms when he ran. The muscles that ran along his upper arms and across his shoulders were lethal looking. Of course, watching the powerful cords of strength in his legs ripple and bulge was a fascinating pastime as well. She'd frequently found herself wishing that he ran a little slower. There never seemed to be enough time to see it all. She had finally taken to watching his arms one day and his legs the next.

Suddenly the man turned and, stepping lively in place, checked the traffic before running out into the street.

"Oh," Emily said with a gasp. "He's crossing the street. He's coming this way. He's coming here."

"Good. Now I can get a better look at him."

"Oh, Jennifer, please, don't look at him," Emily said, agitated. "I mean, well, you can look at him, but don't stare or draw his attention to us. Please."

"Why not?"

"Because. Please. I'm begging."

Jennifer rolled her eyes and adjusted herself so

that she could appear to be deeply into selecting wallpaper and spy on the jogger at the same time. Actually she was quite good at this sort of covert operation and probably would have done it even if Emily hadn't asked.

The bell on the door jingled as the man came in. Emily caught the briefest glimpse of his face before he took up the towel from around his neck and hid his appearance, wiping the sweat from his brow.

"Aw," Jennifer groaned disappointedly.

"Shh." Emily wasn't disappointed. He seemed almost larger than life to her close up, which made for a lot more rippling muscle to see. She was a patient woman. She could content herself with thick, long, sinewy legs and broad, brawny shoulders until she discovered the rest of what went with the dark hair that curled so charmingly along the nape of his neck when it was damp with perspiration.

Emily and Jennifer stood motionless over their sample books, straining to hear what the man was saying to the storekeeper at the back of the shop. He was apparently looking for something specific that wasn't in stock and was being genial over his lack of success. The elbow in Emily's ribs was her signal that the man was on his way back to the front of the shop. As if on cue, both women very casually looked up as the jogger reached the door. He turned his head and looked straight at them.

Emily just about died. Her heart stopped. Respiration ceased. Even her nervous system degenerated to a spastic jumble of sporadic impulses as she took in warm brown eyes, a thin, noble nose, a high brow, and perfect, kissable lips. For an instant she thought a fly might have zoomed into her open mouth; she closed it with a snap. She watched as his eyes seemed to gobble up Jennifer in one easy swallow. She went to heaven when his gaze met and held hers for one whole glorious second. Then he smiled. Emily's kneecaps melted, and she gripped the display table to keep herself upright.

"Ladies," he said in a voice as deep and rich as King Solomon's mines. He nodded, and just like that opened the door and was gone.

"Isn't he wonderful," Emily said in awe, her voice a bare whisper.

"Yeah. Wonderful." Jennifer didn't sound too impressed. "Who is he?"

"I don't know. I haven't met him," Emily said absently, leaning over the table to watch the jogger until he was out of sight. "He runs past the house every day at eight o'clock sharp." She gasped and turned to look at Jennifer. "He's late today, but I'll bet that's where he's going now."

"For crying out loud, Emily. He's a half-naked man who's sweaty and probably smelly as well; you don't know his name or who he is or how much money he makes, and you're acting as if he's . . . as if he's somebody special."

"Oh, I think he must be," Emily said quietly. "Or at least, I think he is."

Jennifer closed her eyes and shook her head in hopelessness. "I thought we'd already been through all this," she said in her you-poor-demented-Emily voice as she turned back to the table piled high with samples of wall coverings. "See this book of wallpaper samples?" She flipped open a book at random and fanned the pages rapidly. "Picking out a man is just like picking out wallpaper for your stairwell."

Emily frowned at her in confusion, then frowned

at the catalogue. "That's not exactly been my experience, but if you say so . . ."

"Look at it this way, Emily. There are a zillion patterns to choose from. Just like men. Some you can live with, some you can't. Just like men. Some of those patterns will be out-of-date or unavailable. Just like men. Once you finally settle on one, you take it home and slap it on the wall. If it sticks, you live happily ever after. If it doesn't, you get your money back in a settlement. If you get sick of the pattern, you come back to the store and pick out a new one. It's all very simple and nothing to get excited about, unless . . ."

"Unless what?" Emily was very curious to know what would make one man among zillions special enough to excite Jennifer.

"Well, unless, of course, he was a truly superb lover. Then you'd have something."

"What if he was exceptionally intelligent or witty or sensitive?"

"All three and sexy to boot would probably kill you. But you don't need to worry yourself about that ever happening, honey. That man hasn't been made yet." Jennifer gave Emily a reassuring pat on the shoulder and moseyed off to see if there was anything the least bit interesting to see in the rest of the shop.

"The ultimate romantic," Emily labeled her cousin under her breath as she turned back to the samples. Well, if anyone knew about men, the dark, striking Jennifer certainly should. Married and divorced three times, she was never at a loss for a date when she wanted one. However, in this case she opted to think her cousin's opinion might be slightly warped. She found it very hard to compare the jogger to a piece of wallpaper.

"Look, how about if I just leave you the money

and you come back some other day and pick out your paper," Jennifer suggested, her hands on Emily's shoulders as she turned her toward the door. "I need to get home sometime during this century, and you still haven't told me what you've decided to do about that history professor over at the college."

Emily followed her cousin out the door without an argument. She'd known better than to try to pick out wallpaper with her anyway. Jennifer just wasn't in a wallpaper-picking mood.

"I haven't made up my mind yet," she said a short while later over a light lunch. The small café on Main Street was nearly empty as it was almost two P.M., the time when Jennifer preferred to eat. "I wrote and told this Professor McEntire that most of those stories about old William Joseph were just that, stories. I told him it would be a waste of his time, that dozens of historians had been over and over those papers and found nothing. But he still wants to come to the house and go through all that stuff in the attic."

"Haven't you heard about just saying no?"

"Yes, of course, but he seems very determined."

"Of course he does. You know what he's looking for, don't you?"

"Yes. I know what he's looking for. And you know as well as I do that it isn't there . . . if it ever existed. It wouldn't be fair to lead the professor on by allowing him to start looking for something that just plain isn't there."

"Well, it is his time, honey. If he wants to waste it, let him. Who knows. Maybe his middle name is Lucky."

Emily slipped her cousin a discrediting glance.

William Joseph Becket was her grandfather's grandfather—there were too many *greats* and *grands* in there to describe his relationship to Emily any other way. Rumor had it that old William Joseph had been a very busy man during the Civil War. A diehard Rebel wounded but not incapacitated early on in the war, he was said to have carried on some not so honorable and very treasonous acts in the name of the Confederacy throughout the remaining war years. Not the least of which was harboring a fortune in stolen gold—gold that was never recovered.

Emily had never been too sure if she believed all the stories or not. She liked to imagine the gold was still out there for some clever person like herself to find. But it made more sense to think that if it ever *had* existed, it surely would have been found sometime in the past one hundred years.

"If you were clever, you could arrange to meet this *wonderful* jogger of yours, you know," Jennifer said, catching Emily's undivided attention again as she changed the topic of conversation.

"How?"

"You could take up jogging."

"And fall over dead at his feet by the time I reached the front gates." Emily was about as athletic as an orange.

"Or you could approach him with the idea of giving some exercise classes at that place where you work, 'club dead.' "

"That's not funny, Jennifer."

"Well, honestly, Emily. It's no wonder you don't know how to relate to anyone under the age of seventy. You need a new job."

"I love my job. It's satisfying. I enjoy the work, and I especially enjoy the people." She paused then added, "And please don't call it 'club dead' again."

"Too close to the truth?"

Emily gave her a mordant stare. "Let's talk about something else."

"Okay. We can talk about the Remount Ball if you want. I know you love that."

Emily gave a derisive snort. "It's your turn to go. I went last year."

"You're going again this year. I have plans."

"That's what you said two years ago and I wound up filling in for you then too."

"Well, you're much better at those sort of things than I am, Emily. They're so boring. I swear, the last time I went, I thought I'd contracted a terminal yawn."

"Very funny. But I'm not filling in for you this time."

Jennifer studied her cousin long and hard. Nobody knew Emily better than Jennifer did. When Emily made up her mind about something in that quiet, deliberate way she had about her, there was no changing it. "You come with me, then. I swear, if you don't, I'll do something horribly outrageous to disgrace the family name. I'll bring the press to witness it, and it'll cause such a scandal, they'll have to close the college." Jennifer wasn't above a good threat to get what she wanted.

"Has anyone ever accused you of being a little overdramatic?" Emily asked, stone-faced, already wondering if she could get away with wearing last year's gown.

"Maybe once," she admitted, smiling too sweetly. "But never twice."

Emily sighed. She didn't mind this particular fund-raising affair as much as Jennifer did. It was one of those things that went along with being a big fish in a small pond. But she fully understood why her cousin wasn't willing to go it alone. If misery loved company, so did tedium, embarrassment, and frustration. "Okay. I'll go."

"Good. I'll drive out in the afternoon and dress at the house." Jennifer frowned. "Although I don't know why you didn't insist they have it the same day as your birthday so I wouldn't have to make two trips in the same week."

"I am sorry about that," Emily said, knowing how much Jennifer disliked the inconvenience of having to travel so far to see her. "I didn't have any say in the matter. But I'm still awfully glad you came today."

"Haven't missed your birthday yet, have I?"

"No." Emily smiled. As last living relatives go, Jennifer wasn't such a bad one to have. She was a little self-centered and outspoken. She was cynical and rude sometimes. In fact, Emily had always been glad they were both tall. It would have been very difficult, indeed, to have Jennifer speaking to her and looking down her nose at her at the same time. But in her own way she loved Emily. And Emily loved her.

Their celebratory luncheon came to an end, and the cousins hugged good-bye at Jennifer's car, which was parked outside the café.

"I'll see you Friday, then. And for pity's sake, don't wear that horrible green thing you wore last year. If you have to, use the wallpaper money," Jennifer called through the open window of her car before she drove away, leaving Emily no time to argue. Not that it mattered. They both knew Emily would wear whatever she pleased. But it always seemed to give Jennifer pleasure to have the last word, just in case she could use an I-told-you-so later.

Two

Emily turned and walked slowly toward Becket House. It was her thirtieth birthday. It was two in the afternoon. The day was barely half over, and her birthday had already come to an end. Was that all there was to turning thirty? Somehow, she'd been expecting more—instant dentures, or maybe a wiser, more trustworthy look about herself. Instead, she still felt that . . . almost-thirty feeling. That feeling that time was moving but she wasn't. That the world was changing but she wasn't. That she'd spent enough time on the face of the earth to have everything she needed to be happy and content but she wasn't.

She didn't feel this way often, but something in the fresh spring air dampened her spirits. Emily couldn't shake the feeling that part of her was flapping loosely in the wind, unanchored and dissatisfied. To make things worse, she knew exactly what was missing. Emily wanted to be married. She wanted a husband and children. She didn't think she was wishing for the impossible, although sometimes it sure felt like it.

And it wasn't as though she hadn't ever tried to attain this secret, inner dream of hers. She had. And contrary to anything Jennifer had to say, Emily was no stick-in-the-mud. Her life wasn't the endless party or the constant revolving door that her cousin's was; but then, it didn't have to be.

She'd had a fling or an affair or two in her time, but she'd never really lost her heart. She'd tried to lose it to a balding math teacher whom she thought she had a lot in common with. But what he had defined as "a quiet life by the hearth" was more like a life sentence at a crematorium to Emily. The man had been duller than dull with a dispiriting interest in taxidermy.

Emily shook her head. Dwelling on the past wasn't moving her forward. And now, at the age of thirty, forward was the direction in which she needed to go—and fast. She didn't live the sort of life or in a locale that put her in contact with a lot of eligible men. Her book of wallpaper samples had a very limited selection. If she was to achieve her heart's desire, she was going to have to do something drastic. Move maybe, although she'd hate to leave Becket House.

Emily mentally reviewed her other choices as she walked past the Presbyterian church that stood on the corner of Main and Union streets. She automatically looked at it. Next to Becket House, it was her favorite building in town. She liked the old stained glass windows and the tall steeple. It amazed her that every rock in its walls had been hand forged, cut and laid by a few simple, hard-working religious men who'd wanted a church in their community over a hundred years earlier. Best of all was the antiquated graveyard behind the church. It was full of ancient tombstones in every size and shape imaginable.

Some were very ordinary with simply a name and a date. Some were sad with the mournful words of a mother who had lost her child. Others were almost humorous as they tried to describe in twenty-five words or less the not-so-virtuous life of a drunken husband. Still, there were those that were sweet and loving monuments to cherished partners. Emily took note of some of those she liked best as she made her way to the top of a small hill at the far end of the cemetery.

Inside a plot that was surrounded by a low wrought iron fence lay the remains of generations of Beckets. Her parents, grandparents, even old William Joseph rested quietly there in the old churchyard. Every relative Emily ever had, except Jennifer's mother—who had opted to be buried elsewhere—and, of course, Jennifer, were right there at her feet. In her depressed thirty-year-old frame of mind, the grave site seemed sadder than it ever had before. She usually took great pride in knowing who she was and where she'd come from. It was comforting to know that the family skeletons were not in a closet somewhere, but, rather, slept side by side in the family plot.

But today she was overcome with the impression that she had somehow let her ancestors down. The family name of Becket would die with her. Even the bloodline would be lost if she or Jennifer didn't pass it on eventually. She couldn't hold the melancholy sigh that escaped her at the thought of all the Beckets before her who had fought so hard to stay alive, just to have it all end with her.

For at least the hundredth time she read the words chiseled into William Joseph's stone.

William Joseph Becket
1841–1903
Lived for the good of the South
Died a faithful soldier.

Again, and for the hundredth time, the words puzzled her. According to her grandfather, his grandfather had been a very family-oriented and loving man. He'd dedicated his life to bettering things in the South after the war. It had always seemed a little strange that he'd carried a bitterness toward the North all the way to his grave. He'd been a young man during the war, and things had changed considerably by the time he died. Emily would have thought that by then he would have learned to forgive and forget.

"Impressive, isn't it?"

"Ayah," Emily squeaked, nearly jumping out of her skin in fright. She spun around to face the source of the deep masculine voice that had startled her, only to be shocked once again.

"I'm sorry. I didn't mean to scare you. I thought you heard me coming up behind you," the jogger said. Emily's heart raced from zero to a hundred and fifty beats in a flat second. Her nerves seemed to be hopping up and down. Her body felt like one huge tingle.

She stood staring at him, taking in eyes that were much darker than she had originally thought —darker and deeper and warmer. He was dressed now, she observed, admitting that as nice as his bare muscles were from afar, she preferred he be completely clothed if she was going to speak coherently.

He looked comfortable in his snug blue jeans, which was more than Emily could say about the effect they were having on her. The legs she thought she knew so well looked thicker encased in denim, but no less strong and powerful. His shoulders, too, took on inches under a well-worn brown leather jacket. The white cable-knit sweater he wore beneath it softened the effect a little, but on the whole he was more than merely handsome as he stood before her. Emily shivered.

"Are you all right? You're shaking. I'm really very sorry I disturbed you," he said, deeply concerned. He reached out a hand to comfort and reassure her, but Emily instinctively jumped backward out of harm's way. She was fairly certain that if he touched her, she'd fall into the family plot and take her rightful place there forever. And she wasn't about to do that—yet.

Because suddenly thirty didn't seem old at all. She heard birds singing, and the grass seemed greener, the sky bluer than she had ever seen them before. When violins began to play, Emily shook her head. Too much, she decided. The man definitely did wonderful things to her insides, but she knew he didn't expect her to act like a blithering idiot.

"No. No. I'm fine. You didn't really disturb me," she said nervously, answering all his questions at once now that they'd registered in her brain. "I . . . my mind was someplace else. I wasn't expecting you. . . . I wasn't expecting anyone actually. I . . . well, I'm fine. Really."

The man smiled, taking Emily at her word. She turned the corners of her lips upward and stood there wondering if he was a dentist. His teeth were so straight and so white. And those lips . . . She moaned inwardly, awkwardly shifting her weight from one foot to the other. His mouth was an unsettling masterpiece.

"I saw you in the hardware store earlier, didn't

I?" he asked, obviously trying to put her at ease. Instead, her heart jerked convulsively. That he'd actually remember her standing next to Jennifer in the store thrilled her no end. She wasn't usually the one people remembered. "Do you come here very often?"

"No. Not often." Did she look the sort of person who hung around graveyards? Maybe she *should* get a new coat.

"I love these old cemeteries," he said, glancing around at the tombstones. "There's as much history written here as in any book. Some of these people knew how to get a lot said in very few words."

"Yes, they did. I'm afraid it would take me forever to come up with a decent epitaph. In fact, I've decided to leave mine to my cousin and hope she doesn't go first. She's very clever with words," she told him, and then refused to believe the words had come from her mouth.

"You seem to have given this some thought. I hope you're not planning an early demise."

"Well, not any earlier than necessary. But I don't like putting things off until the last minute." She hadn't said that either, she told herself soothingly.

"That's a wise way to be." Emily didn't miss the humor in his eyes or the way he was holding his smile back, keeping it from turning into a full-blown grin.

But Emily could see no humor in the situation. Here she was, alone with the most beautiful man she'd ever seen, talking about death. Jennifer would disown her if she heard about it.

"I'm not always like this, you know," she felt compelled to tell him. "I think of other things besides dying. Today's my birthday. I was thinking about that too." The sound of her own voice echoed through her ears. Was she possessed? She desperately hoped the man would think so and leave her to commit emotional hara-kiri. She couldn't remember ever sounding so dim-witted.

"So, I caught you in the middle of a life evaluation, huh? Well, happy birthday, and how has your life fared so far?"

He didn't appear to be making fun of her. His expression was open and friendly and interested. He was either being extremely polite and ignoring the inappropriateness of the conversation, or he was a very tolerant person who would discuss anything with anybody, she thought. For a moment Emily looked at him as though he were a close, trusted friend. But when he shoved his hands into the back pockets of his jeans, pulling the material tightly across his lower torso, waiting for her answer, she quickly recalled who he was—a handsome stranger. Still, that didn't mean she had to lie to him.

"Not too bad," she said candidly. "I have a good life even though it's not everything I had hoped it would be by now. But overall, I'm pretty content with it." The man nodded his understanding and smiled at her. She sensed a feeling of approval from him, but she didn't know why. "What about your life. In general, I mean. Are you happy with it?"

He gave her question some consideration before answering. "Yeah. I am happy with it. Most of the time. I think everybody has some *what if's* in their lives, but for the most part, I'm pretty content with things."

Emily nodded. This was one of the deepest, most intimately personal conversations she'd ever had with a man, and she didn't even know his name. Something told her the situation was very odd, but it didn't feel that way. The man was open and honest and easy to talk to. The only thing about him that made her uncomfortable was his incredible body, and she suspected that was because she was deeply in lust with it. If he were old or ugly, she could be completely at ease with him. As it was . . .

A long, empty silence stretched between them. Emily wanted to ask if his contentment with life had anything to do with his wife but couldn't think of a way to say it without sounding too obvious. Why couldn't she have inherited some of old William Joseph's cleverness? She slipped a glance over at her relative's headstone, admonishing him for being so stingy.

"Do you, ah, know the Beckets?" the man asked suddenly with a vague hand gesture toward the family plot. "Not these Beckets, of course, but do you know Emily Becket?"

"Yes. I do," she said, debating whether or not to tell him who she was. There was something romantic about meeting mysteriously and anonymously in a graveyard. Emily would have given anything to have a fog bank roll in around them. "This is a small town. Nearly everyone knows her. And, actually, I *did* know a couple of these people." She didn't want to have to tell him any fibs or pretend that she wasn't Emily, so she directed the conversation back to the dead Beckets.

"Not that one, though, right?" he asked, indicating William Joseph's grave.

"Before my time."

"Do you think all the stories about him are true?"

"Truth?"

"Mmm."

"I don't know. Folks around here like to believe

them and pass them on to everyone who comes to town. It's our claim to fame. But sometimes I think my—I think they would have found the treasure long ago if there was ever one to find. Historians and reporters have been crawling all over this place since after the war, even before old William died. They would have turned up something by now, don't you think?"

"Maybe." He didn't seem to think this was necessarily so. "What's this Emily Becket like?"

"Emily? Oh, she's just a regular person."

"Hmm." He seemed to have his own opinion about her. Naturally, Emily's curiosity was piqued.

"Why do you ask?"

"Well, she's the one I've come all the way from Philadelphia to meet, and she's proving to be very elusive."

"Emily Becket? Elusive?"

"Yeah. When I call, she never answers. I write letters, and she puts me off. You'd think she was an eccentric old recluse. But I've heard she spends a lot of time at the senior citizens' center here. I even tried to meet her there, but they said she hadn't come in that day."

"Old?" she asked as if it were the only word she'd heard. If he'd gone to the center and she hadn't seen him, that only meant it had been her day off. But old?

"I was told she was a spinster."

"A spinster?" Emily could actually feel herself becoming drawn and haggard.

"Well, it doesn't matter anyway," he went on. "I understand that it's practically mandatory that she show up at the Remount Ball. I'll make my move on her then."

Visions of sugarplums danced in her head as she considered the endless possibilities of the kinds of moves he'd be making on her when next they met. However, she was sure that none of them had even crossed his mind.

"Will you, by any chance, be attending the ball?" she heard him ask.

"Ah, yes. I'll be there."

"Good. I have to be going, but I'll look for you at the ball. Okay?" he said, smiling at Emily in a way that made her think of roses and whispered promises.

"Okay," she said, knowing that she sounded too eager. She watched him walk away and groaned at the sleek, fluid way he walked. He was even better to watch from behind than he was from the side. And she still didn't know his name. She thought about calling out and asking who he was, then decided that there would be time enough to find out when he presented himself to the old spinster lady, Emily Becket. For now she wanted things to remain as they were. He, the mysterious and handsome stranger in town, and she, the not-so-old, enigmatic woman from the graveyard.

Three

During the course of the afternoon Emily drifted slowly back to earth. All she could think about was her meeting with the gorgeous jogger. Recalling the timbre of his voice and the way he'd looked at her with his deep chocolate-brown eyes would send her free-floating until she didn't know if she was up, down, or sideways.

It was during one of her brief touchdowns that she thought to wonder why he'd come all the way from Philadelphia to see her. And when had she ever received a letter from him? Surely she would have remembered. On second thought, maybe she wouldn't have. Unless he'd signed it "the beautiful jogger," she might not have realized who it was from.

Leafing through the day's mail, she found nothing but bills and ads. The only thing she could come up with, in recent memory, was her correspondence with the history professor from the college, McEntire. Never having met him, she hadn't exactly pictured him as her jogger. Professor McEntire's letters conjured up visions of an all-business, middle-age man with printer's ink on his nose, a bald spot on the back of his head, stooped shoulders, and a history text permanently affixed to his right hand. A far cry from the robust, windblown, and unencumbered jogger.

Still, it was the only likely conclusion she could come up with, given her somewhat diminished mental capacity. It didn't really matter anyway. If he was this McEntire person, she'd see him again at the fund-raiser. She could tell him once and for all to his face that there was nothing of any interest or value to him in her attic. And if he wasn't the professor, so much the better. She could discover then why he'd been trying to reach her. Either way, she was going to see him once more, and the thought sent her spirits soaring.

The day of the Remount Ball arrived. The sun was shining brightly, even though the cool spring breezes continued to chill the air.

"He didn't come by this morning," Emily told her cousin, drawing back the old lace curtain from the window for the twentieth time since Jennifer had arrived an hour before.

"Maybe he tripped and broke his leg." Jennifer sounded hopeful. She was obviously growing perturbed with Emily's preoccupation with the runner.

"Well, I'm hoping he had something else to do this morning and will come by this afternoon. It's cool enough so he wouldn't get overheated."

"Emily, honey, I thought you wanted him overheated."

Emily cast her cousin an exasperated look and moved away from the window, disappointed. All week she'd made sure that she was in place to watch him run past the house before she left for work. She'd been careful not to draw attention to herself by wiggling the curtains or going outside until he was long gone. She preferred to live in her own little fantasy land for as long as possible. She liked to pretend that she had somehow bewitched him completely in the cemetery and that he was as eager to meet her again at the ball as she was to see him up close again. In her dreams she plagued his mind and destroyed his appetite. Soon enough he'd find out who she was and that she had nothing to offer him. In the meantime, what harm could a little deluding do?

"You know, if you were clever, you'd come up with a way of meeting him and holding his attention for a while," Jennifer said, breaking in on Emily's sweet imaginings. "It shouldn't be too hard. Jocks are usually dumber than doorknobs, and you're a very smart girl. Forget the first three buttons on your blouses and go braless. The poor man won't know what hit him."

"Oh, right, Jennifer. That's so totally me," she said facetiously. "Why don't I just run through the streets naked and see what happens?"

"Well, where has being totally you gotten you so far, Emily? Sometimes you have to put forth a little effort to get what you want. Change a little. Take risks. Although, in your case, I wouldn't call going braless terribly risky."

Emily declined to argue this particular point and instead tried to create a diversion. "What could I possibly do to keep his interest once I've met him. I'm not athletic, health food gives me diarrhea, and even though my work suits me just fine, it can't be all that stimulating to someone else."

"Oh, you'd think of something. There's always

something, and like I said, you're a smart girl. You'd find it."

Jennifer's confidence in her was inspiring. So was the dress she'd bought with her wallpaper money. That evening, in the low-cut black silk gown with the rhinestone trim, she looked slim and sleek. The little peplum at her waist was romantic and warded off any impression of her being too skinny. She felt sexy and sensual, noticing curves she hadn't realized she owned. Her nondescript brown hair, which she usually kept braided and under control, now glimmered with golden highlights as it fell in soft curls to her shoulders. She smiled in approval at her reflection in the mirror. She'd never thought of herself as someone a man would look twice at, but this dress made her *feel* beautiful. Her shy puritan nature could certainly withstand a jolt once in a while, she decided.

"Now, where's that jogger when we're ready for him?" Jennifer wanted to know as she circled Emily with a critical eye. "Isn't it just like a man not to be around when you could knock him dead with your eyelashes?"

"You like it, then?"

"Of course I like it. You're beautiful, Emily. Now we look like cousins." Emily was flattered indeed.

It wasn't until after she'd arrived at the somewhat snooty soiree, held in the elegant old library of the college, that she began to wonder if she'd miscalculated the timing in her change of appearance.

"Emily dear," gushed Judith Windtharp, corpulent wife of the dean of students. "You bought a new dress." Unsure of how to respond, Emily remained silent, growing warmer and more self-conscious by the minute. "You look lovely, dear. Really. The change is very refreshing."

From that point on, Emily found eye contact with other familiar trustees and benefactors all but impossible. She was so aware of herself and the way she looked that she felt as if they were staring at her whether they were or not. Were they all taking note of the change in poor Emily? Had she presented herself so badly before?

Nursing a glass of white wine, she mingled among the crowd of well-educated, well-endowed alumni, and "friends of the college," as Judith Windtharp had a tendency to call them. Over and over again she was called upon to identify herself as the great-great-granddaughter of the founder of the college and explain his reasons for championing the cause of higher education in the South nearly a hundred years earlier.

Emily hadn't the foggiest idea what had possessed her ancestor to do the things he did, but over the years and after what seemed like a zillion of these fund-raising affairs, she'd developed a set of pat answers that always seemed to please people and generate the money needed.

"Is it true that your ancestor was a slave owner?" one young woman with a decidedly northern accent asked in gruesome interest.

"No," Emily answered, taking no offense. "I think he would have liked to have owned a few and probably would have if he could have afforded it. But the truth is, he was a poor dirt farmer before the war. He had a wife and children whom he just barely managed to take care of. He worked his land alone. It was hard work, and he lost huge amounts of his crops because he had no help at harvest time." She shrugged. "But that's the way it was back then. The poor stayed poor and the rich got richer. Sound familiar?" she asked, smiling good-naturedly. It was only natural that people would be curious about such a strong character as old William Joseph.

"Did any of his children go to school here?" asked an older gentleman.

"He had two sons, who were educated at home by their mother, who got her education through the church and was a schoolteacher herself for several years before marrying my great-great-grandfather. The first Becket to attend school here was William Joseph's grandson. I think he wound up being a banker or some such thing. And several more of us were educated here since then. So, you see, we do practice what we preach."

The crowd around her laughed at her little joke, as they always did, and another question was posed. Emily drew comfort in knowing that Jennifer was trapped somewhere in the room, answering a similar set of questions.

There was food lavishly laid out everywhere. The crowd was merry and gay. Music filled the room, and laughter floated on the air high above the book-lined balcony and into every corner of the magnificent marble-floored hall. Emily had always been a little amazed at how huge the room truly was when the usual tables and chairs were removed. And she'd always thought it the most appropriate room on the campus to hold functions in because the endless rows of books lent an air of permanence and history and wisdom to the occasions.

One of the few things she enjoyed about these parties was the sense of continuity she invariably experienced sometime during the evening. Knowing that a Becket had always been present since the opening day ceremonies over which her great-great-grandmother, Maggie Becket, had presided gave Emily much comfort and a feeling of being immortal. Somehow it was nice to know that even after she was gone, her name would live on on the lips of future generations.

Emily sighed. Surrounded by people, immortalized in mind, tempted to cheerfulness by good food and sweet songs, she was very downhearted. An hour and a half had passed since her arrival, and there hadn't been a glimpse of the jogger—or Professor McEntire. The dress wasn't enough to keep her spirits buoyed. Would she never know the jogger's identity? Would she ever see him again? He hadn't gone running that day. Was he hurt? She became suspicious. Had he really meant to come tonight or had he been leading her on? Was he some sort of cad who played with a woman's emotions and left her hanging?

"Emily. Emily honey." Jennifer's highly excited voice cut through the general din of the crowd like a knife. Emily turned toward her. Her cousin looked as if she'd eaten the canary and won the state lottery all at once. "I have met the most interesting man, a wonderful dancer. But it appears that it's you he's come here to meet." She pushed her way through the small group of people surrounding her cousin with the man in tow. With a flick of her dainty wrist she brought him into the foreground for presentation. "Emily, this is Professor McEntire. My cousin, Emily Becket."

The man looked surprised. Emily was stunned. Not because of his identity but because he was even more breathtakingly handsome in a white dinner jacket than she had ever seen him before. She relished the secret knowledge that the width and breadth of his shoulders had nothing to do with the artistic handiwork of a tailor.

"You're Emily Becket?" he asked, not displeased but needing to be sure.

She extended her hand to him in the guise of friendship, but there was more than friendship on her mind. She reached out with the need to touch him, to verify his realness. "Professor McEntire. I've been looking forward to meeting you." She was very proud of the fact that her voice sounded calm and perfectly normal.

"And I you," he said in a low voice. The intensity of his eyes as they took in her new dress—or more to the point, what her new dress left revealed —gave her the distinct impression that his interest in her went beyond her great-great-grandfather's papers. Then again, she cautioned herself, dark eyes often seemed deeper and more probing because of their color, and they could be deceptive.

"Ah, have you met . . ." She introduced him to those standing around them, very conscious of the hand that came to her elbow to keep her close by as the professor leaned in front of her to shake hands with the other guests. His aftershave made her senses reel, but still she breathed deeper. Who made men like him, she wondered in a dreamlike state of euphoria.

"A professor of history, no doubt," she heard one of the older alumni guess in a jovial manner. "Come to discover the treasure of Becket House, huh?"

He laughed lightly. "Actually, I'm a law professor. And," he said, turning his chocolate-brown gaze on Emily once more, "I think I've already found the treasure of Becket House."

Oh, heavens! Emily was at a total loss. She knew this called for a snappy, clever comeback.

And she knew she was staring at him with her mouth open. But she couldn't seem to help herself. The man took her breath away and turned her brain to a bog. She shot a quick, beseeching glance at Jennifer, who grinned and wagged her eyebrows. There was nothing witty written across the toes of her shoes. Seconds were passing. She had to say something. Finally Emily felt she had no recourse but to blurt out the first thing that came to mind. "Would you care to dance, Professor McEntire?"

"I'd be honored," he said without batting an eye, smiling at Emily as if she'd just paid him a great compliment. Emily wanted to die.

"Very nice," Jennifer muttered under her breath as she passed behind her cousin. "Be aggressive. Bring him to his knees."

That wasn't at all what Emily wanted to do. She liked the way he stood tall and erect. She liked the way he held his shoulders back, proud and confident. She'd asked him to dance only because she wanted to be in his arms, just once. That wasn't aggression, it was a decided weakness on her part.

If she'd inadvertently done any damage to his pride, however, it certainly didn't show. He was still smiling when he took her hand and excused them from the group. He led her through the throng of people toward the band and found a dark, secluded corner, where he took her into his arms. It was just as she had imagined it would be. She felt a sudden rebirth in her faith in Santa Claus, the tooth fairy, and dreams come true.

It took her a few minutes to adjust herself to his slow, easy dance pattern. Normally it would have taken her only a second or two, but she was distracted by the heady scent of his cologne and with the way her hand felt engulfed in his much larger grasp. Then, too, she had to get used to the feel of the muscles in his shoulders as they rippled under her fingertips. It was an absorbing sensation.

When she could finally look into his face, she saw that he was still smiling. There was pleasure in his eyes, and he was grinning the way Jennifer had a short time earlier. "I am so glad you're Emily Becket," he said, the relief in his voice underscoring his odd comment.

"Then you're not angry that I didn't tell you the other day, in the cemetery."

"No. But when I didn't see you when I first came in, I was a little worried that you might not come. Thank heaven Emily Becket *had* to come."

"You could have asked almost anyone here; they could have pointed me out for you."

"Yes, but I didn't know who you were then. And when I started looking for Emily Becket, I was looking for someone . . . regular."

"And old and spinsterish," she added, teasing, surprised to find herself talking to him so easily.

"You could hardly be described by either of those adjectives." His hand moved lightly up her back, and she broke out in goose pimples all over her body. "And when I finally asked someone who William Joseph's great-great-granddaughter was, they pointed out your cousin. That's when I knew 'old spinster lady' didn't quite fit."

"And she's not at all regular," Emily said on a note of loving admiration for her cousin.

He looked over her head, and she watched as his dark gaze sought out and found Jennifer. His expression was thoughtful, then he shrugged and looked down at her, saying, "Maybe not, but she's a whole lot closer to regular than you are."

Did the wonders of this man never cease? Brown eyes made a close-up inspection of her face, hair, and her never-before-seen-in-public cleavage. His gaze returned several times to her lower lip, which she automatically slipped between her teeth because she was nervous. Her skin grew very warm, and her knees began to tingle as minutes passed while they swayed in each other's arms, not speaking but communicating nonetheless.

"What are you really like, Emily Becket?" he finally asked, his voice barely a whisper. He was asking the same question with his eyes and with his hands as they took a slightly firmer grip, pulling her closer to him.

Emily's thinly veiled breasts brushed lightly against the fine material that covered his chest. She felt herself engorge and prickle into hard points, and she yearned to repeat the experience. She fought an urge to cover her chest with her arms in fear of showing how affected she was. But it wasn't much of a battle. She was fast approaching the point of not caring how big a fool she made of herself.

This was one night out of her whole life. One night when she could do anything she wanted to. Wear a plunging neckline. Look sexy as hell. Speak exactly what she thought. Drool over the most gorgeous man on earth and dance in his arms. What harm could one night of living in a dream do?

"I'm just like everyone else," she said. Only tonight she was a mankiller, a sexpot!

"I don't believe you."

Looking into his eyes, Emily envisioned herself drowning in a vat of hot fudge. "It's true. I'm just regular folk." She wanted to throw him to the ground and give him a regular and thorough ravishment. Every time his pelvis brushed lightly against hers, the muscles in her lower abdomen curled and shivered with anticipation.

"Okay, be mysterious. I love a good riddle."

She laughed softly and gave him what she hoped was a teasing smile. If he knew how truly ordinary she was, he'd be very disappointed. And she didn't want that to happen. Not this night, anyway. There was time enough for him to discover she wasn't rich or exotic like Jennifer. There was plenty of time for him to find out that she was a quiet little homebody who worked for a living and derived great pleasure from serving others.

"Did you attend Remount College?" he asked with no great interest in the answer other than as a place to start his investigation.

"Yes. I was a sociology major."

He nodded. "And do you use your degree?"

"Yes." It was plain that he was expecting her to elaborate, but in keeping with her newfound mysteriousness, she remained silent, smiling sweetly.

The professor's eyes narrowed keenly as he studied her face for clues. His lips turned up at the corners. He was enjoying his mental maneuvers. When his face suddenly lit with inspiration, Emily gasped at its brilliance. She liked the way he spoke with his eyes, the way his lips stretched across even white teeth when he smiled, and the deep, throaty chuckle that indicated his amusement.

"The senior citizens' center. Right?"

Emily nodded. "I do spend a lot of time there," she said, reminding him of their conversation in the cemetery. "But I'm not one of the clients."

"Obviously." He'd grown serious and continued to peruse her face with great interest. "You have beautiful eyes," he said. Emily didn't actually hear him say she had beautiful eyes, he spoke too softly to be heard over the music. But his lips fascinated her, and she'd seen the words form there as if his thoughts had escaped him one syllable at a time.

"They're brown," she said, painfully self-conscious. She felt like an alien in her own body. Eyes that she had always taken for granted were now orbs of stunning delight.

"I know," he said softly but audibly this time. "They're a very unusual brown, and they show so much of what you're feeling."

Oh, dear. "They do?" she questioned, dismayed. If he could see what she was thinking . . .

"It's easy to tell when you're happy or excited. They turn almost a gold color." Emily had a feeling they were shining like pyrite at the moment. She and the magnificent jogger were stepping smoothly together in a small circle on the dance floor, staring into each other's eyes. It soon became evident to Emily that wishing wasn't always a waste of time.

He shook his head as if trying to bring himself back to reality, and grinned down at her sheepishly. "I feel like a jerk. I can't remember the last time a woman's affected me the way you have."

Who? Me? Emily's mind went completely blank.

"I'm sorry. I've embarrassed you," he said when she couldn't bring herself to speak coherently but stood staring at him instead. "I didn't mean to. I . . . it's just that after I left you in the cemetery the other day . . . well, I was a block away before I realized that I didn't even know your name. I went back, but you were gone. I got this horrible feeling that I'd never see you again, and . . . I'm really sorry."

"No," she said simply, testing her vocal cords for stability. "Don't be sorry. I'm very flattered." She was flabbergasted, but this was no time to split hairs. She wanted to hear more of what he had to say about her.

"Emily, is that big brute dancin' you too hard? You look positively breathless, honey." Jennifer's voice invaded their world much like a troop of marines on field maneuvers.

Flustered, Emily began to move, following the professor's lead. Her heart was racing, and she *was* breathless. She felt as if she were at the tail end of a marathon dance—and she hadn't even been moving.

"The professor is a wonderful dancer," she said, trying to sound normal. Jennifer was dancing with the chairman of the board of trustees of the college. It wouldn't do at all to start blithering like a tongue-tied teenager. "I do think it's a little crowded and stuffy in here, though. Have we ever had this large a crowd before, Mr. Macky?" Emily asked, thinking it was a good way to get out of the spotlight. Amos Macky could talk a person's face off, given a good subject, and money always worked best.

The man droned on and on for what seemed like forever, but this time Emily didn't mind at all. She memorized her dance partner's features until she knew them as well as she knew her own. Thick black lashes framed the dark, intuitive eyes that she was so attracted to. There was a thin, pale scar not a half-inch long over his right cheekbone. It was so small, she wouldn't have noticed it if she hadn't been so close to him. His ears were well-shaped too. She wasn't an ear person, but everything about the man fascinated her. Thanks to Amos Macky, she could soak in all his finer details unnoticed. And all she had to do in return was nod at Amos now and again as if she were listening.

"We haven't really had a chance to discuss it yet, Amos," she heard the professor say before he turned his ardent gaze on her. "We were just getting to know each other better."

"That's right," she agreed, thinking faster than she ever had before. "We'll probably discuss it later." Whatever *it* was, she added mentally, smiling sweetly at Amos.

"Now, don't give this young man a hard time of it, Emily," Amos Macky said. "I've known his family almost as long as I've known yours. I assured him that you wouldn't object to his seeing those old papers of your ancestor's. You aren't going to make a liar out of me, are you?"

She looked up at the professor, who seemed eager to hear her answer. But even as the thought crossed her mind that he had ulterior motives, he frowned and said, "We can talk business anytime, Amos. Tonight we'd rather dance." His gaze never left Emily's face.

"Lordy. I don't know why anyone would want to dance in this awful crush. There's more room out on the terrace. And it's cooler," Jennifer declared in her not-so-subtle way. Her grinning and winking didn't prevent Emily from feeling embarrassed either. She meant well. The happiness she felt for Emily twinkled in her eyes. She was just having a little problem with her tact.

"Actually, I think I'd like something to drink," Emily said, wishing she and the professor were alone on a desert island. All she wanted to do was look at him, and she didn't appreciate all the interruptions.

They excused themselves, and she followed the professor's tall, muscled body through the crowded room to the bar. He ordered a gin and tonic for himself and Emily asked for a club soda. She didn't want anything to haze her memory of this night.

"Are you still angry that Amos brought up those papers?" he asked, looking out over the crowd for a place for them to sit down and be alone for a while.

"I wasn't angry."

"Well, you weren't too happy about it. I could tell."

"My eyes?"

He looked down at her and grinned. Then he nodded. His search was apparently fruitful because his hand slipped into hers, and he once again began to lead her through the throng of people to a destination only he could see.

"I really wasn't angry. I just don't know what you think you'll find. That stuff has been gone over time and time again. One fool thought it was all in some sort of code. He was at it for months before he finally decided that it was simply an old man's logging of weather conditions, crop results, and local happenings during and after the war. And we told him that before he started."

Amazingly enough, he'd found an empty alcove not far from the french doors that led out onto the terrace, which looked out over the campus commons. They sat on the settee, careful to keep a proper distance between them. Not that they were worried about appearances. It was more a mutual, nonverbal agreement to stay out of the other's personal space until their business relationship was clearly defined.

"Maybe if I explain my reasons for wanting to see them, it might make more sense to you," he said in earnest. Emily gave him her full attention, not that he hadn't had it all along.

"I want to see William Joseph's papers for purely

personal reasons. I'm not a legitimate historian, although I've done some extensive research on the Civil War. It's more of a hobby with me. I won't write about the papers. I just want to read them."

"But why?" she asked, still confused. "If you know of their existence, then you've probably already read all there is to know about them."

He looked at Emily and then at the swirls in the marble floor. When he looked back at her, she could see that he'd made some sort of decision.

"Emily. I'm from an old Philadelphia family. Believe it or not, we have all sorts of old junk in our attic too. And . . . I also had an ancestor who fought in the Civil War. For the Union." He waited for this to settle in her mind before he went on. "Whereas William Joseph came out of the war as a wounded hero with a mysterious legend of covert activities behind him, my great-great-grandfather was court-martialed and came home in disgrace."

"Why? What did he do?"

"He *lost* a major payroll shipment."

Emily frowned. How did someone lose a payroll shipment? In those days most of the soldiers were paid in gold coin. A shipment like that would be heavy and bulky and very hard to misplace. That is, unless . . . it was stolen.

"But there's never been any proof that William Joseph took or hid that money," she said, instantly defensive, not knowing why she felt so strongly about it. "It was a rumor. That's all."

"Yes, but where there are rumors—" he started, but she cut him off before he could finish maligning her great-great-grandfather.

"He would have written it down. Good Lord, he wrote down everything else. How fat his pigs were. How many bushels of apples he picked. He even wrote down the price he got for them. Surely, if he'd stolen thousands of dollars' worth of federal gold, he'd have jotted it down somewhere."

"Would he? Maybe he did. But not in a way that anyone would notice. They say he was a very clever and crafty fellow." He made the description sound more like praise than condemnation, which took the edge off some of Emily's anger.

"Please don't tell me that you think it's in code," she pleaded dramatically, teasing him with her soft laughter.

His easy chuckle was good-natured, and the appreciation in his eyes sent a sizzling jolt of pleasure through her heart.

"No, I don't think it's in code," he told her in a like manner. "And I'm not trying to malign your great-great-grandfather's character. I was curious about the papers and wanted to read them. But I can certainly understand your reluctance to have yet another stranger shuffling through your family history."

Emily sighed in defeat, even though she'd won the battle. How could she possibly deny him anything, she wondered weakly, looking at his strong, handsome face. And if she did, what excuse could she use to see him again? Having dead Civil War veterans in their families was about all they had in common. She wanted—needed—more time with him.

"Can I think about it?" she asked, stalling for time, holding on to her ace.

"Of course. I'm a little sorry it even came up tonight. The last thing I wanted to discuss with my mystery woman was the past. I'm a lot more interested in the present. And in the future." His eyes had a bottomless quality to them that made Emily feel as if she were caught in a vacuum. Her heart beat wildly, and there didn't seem to be any air in the room.

Her nervousness must have been obvious, and the professor must have known that she was about to ask him to dance again. He saved her the awkward advance, seeming to sense from before that it wasn't her style. He held out his hand to her without saying a word, and she took it, ever eager for his slightest touch. Keeping her close by his side and showing an uncanny ability for steering clear of people who might wish to speak with her, he led her back to the dance floor.

She couldn't remember a night passing by so quickly. Nor could she recall ever liking so much the slow, easy instrumentals the musicians played at these affairs. The music forced her to spend the rest of the night in his arms, because they soon discovered that when they weren't dancing it was impossible to be alone. It was a strain on Emily's nervous system, but she managed to bear it.

They did talk some, or, rather, he did. And even though she hung on his every word, she could remember very little in retrospect. She was impressed with his background and with the idea that a Harvard Law School graduate who taught business law at Princeton also ran a small legal aid clinic in south Philly, because, as he put it, "the law is for everyone not just for those who can afford to pay for it." She could recall him being quite adamant on this subject, but when he'd talked about the rest, it was as if he were reading his résumé.

Actually Emily was inspired by his conversational skills. Keeping a dialogue personally impersonal wasn't easy. Then again, lawyers were supposed to be able to talk on and on and never really say anything meaningful, weren't they? At least that's what Jennifer always said about the attorneys who'd managed her divorces.

Well, anyway, Professor McEntire did a fine job of filling in all the long silences that Emily continually left void because she was caught up in the heady euphoria his closeness induced.

"Emily?" The word was soft and sweet on his lips, like warm honey on toast.

"Yes?"

"The music's over. I think the musicians are leaving now."

Her head turned a full two hundred and seventy degrees as she quickly scanned the room. The enormous library was nearly empty, save a few scattered groups of partygoers and the clean-up committee. "Oh, dear," she said with a groan, feeling foolish. "I've kept you here too long. You must be exhausted."

"Not at all. In fact, I've been hoping your cousin would leave with the rest of them, so I could take you home, but she seems determined to wait for you."

"Jennifer's still here?" She looked around again and found her cousin trapped in deep conversation with Amos Macky. The stiff, grimacelike smile on her lips was all the evidence Emily needed to know Jennifer wasn't as happy as she was.

"I should go," she said, her reluctance to leave him having nothing to do with facing Jennifer's anger. "I've had a wonderful time."

"Me too." His voice was soft as he looked deep into her eyes. "May I call you?"

"Yes. Of course." She sounded too eager, but she'd been making a fool of herself all night, and she just couldn't help herself. Thankfully he didn't seem to mind.

Unsure of what to do next, Emily acted on impulse. She stuck her hand out for a friendly goodbye shake. She knew it would be anticlimactic at this point, but she couldn't think of anything else to do short of physically attacking him.

He took her outstretched hand in a delightfully warm clasp, and then in awe she watched as he bent and placed the sweetest kiss of her existence smack on her lips. Emily quickly swallowed the tiny little scream of glee in her throat, giving him a simple smile of pleasure instead.

"Good night, Emily," he said.

"Good night." She sighed.

Four

"For crying out loud, Emily. Will you stop that?" Jennifer ordered peevishly.

"What?"

"It was bad enough that you left me to listen to that moron Macky go on and on about debts and tuition last night. I think the least you could do this morning is spare me the sighs. At least let me finish my coffee before you do it again." Jennifer was not a morning person. She'd spent the night at Becket House after the fund-raiser at the college. Of course, she'd planned to leave earlier and drive back to Richmond the night before, but she didn't want to leave Emily "to stagger home in a lovesick daze."

That's what she'd said, anyway. But Emily knew better. Any one of a dozen people at the party would have given her a safe ride home. Jennifer just wanted to hear all there was to hear about the jogging professor.

"Sorry," Emily said, even though she couldn't control the sighs. The sun was too bright, the sky was too blue. There were birds chirping, and flowers were blooming everywhere. She was in love, and that was more than enough to make a girl sigh.

It didn't matter that it was spring. That the birds would sing and flowers would bloom and the sun would shine in a bright blue sky no matter what. What counted to Emily was that she was taking keen notice of these wonderful things for the first time in ages. Even being thirty was wonderful.

"Did I make a complete ass of myself last night?" Emily asked, risking her cousin's sharp before-noon tongue.

"Not that I noticed," she said, yawning. "I looked more like a fool than you did. But it was your fault."

"Why? What did I do?"

"Oh," she drawled. "You just floated by me while I was trying to get your attention to let you know I was leaving, and you wouldn't even look at me."

"I wasn't drooling, was I?"

"No. I heard you telling him about working in D.C. before your folks died. So, it's my guess you also told him about starting your club . . . for old people," she said, recalling Emily's warning not to call it "club dead" again. Emily didn't make many demands, but when she did she meant them. And Jennifer had learned a long time before, the hard way, that Emily could be very forceful and stubborn when she wanted to be.

Emily sighed again, this time in relief. "So, I was actually speaking coherently, then? I wasn't just jabbering and slobbering all over the front of my dress?"

"Of course not. If you had been, I'd have left immediately—and without telling you. In fact, considering the state you were in at that store the other day, I thought you were behaving with a great deal of control last night."

Emily was beginning to feel better and better. Not only had she spent a memorable night with Professor McEntire, but she hadn't made as big an idiot of herself as she'd thought.

"Oh, Jennifer," she said, dunking one end of her banana in her hot chocolate before biting it off. "I feel like such a jerk when I'm around him. I'm tongue-tied and nervous and awkward. It's as if I've never been around a man before."

"Well, just which one of the very strange assortment of two-legged animals you've gone out with are you calling a man?"

"Jennifer!" Emily wasn't sure whether she was indignant because Jennifer was right or because she was wrong in her description of the men in Emily's life. She just knew that it didn't sound good. For her or the gentlemen.

"Emily, face it. You've never dated anyone who was your equal. You're too soft-hearted. You pick the ugliest, saddest, most down-and-out-looking man in a room and draw him into a conversation because you feel sorry for the beast. I've seen you do it a hundred times." She paused and watched with disgust as Emily dunked her banana in her drink again before eating it. "Occasionally you stumble over one with a spine, and he asks you out on a date, and there you are"—she flipped her hand out in Emily's direction—"out with a very strange person."

Emily didn't think this was the case, but something in her cousin's words did ring true. She had been out with some men that were very . . . different. Then again, she'd never been or ever wanted to be interested in the plastic, stereotypical yuppies and Ivy Leaguers Jennifer seemed to attract. Wasn't there a happy medium?

"*And*," said Jennifer, "you spend the rest of your time with people old enough to be your grandparents. I'm not at all surprised that you don't know what to do with this McEntire person."

She knew she'd probably live to regret it, but Emily had to ask. "What should I do with him?"

Her cousin gave her a silly little smile as if she were dealing with a forgetful child.

"Emily, honey, if the man makes you feel good, and you want him, go out and get him." Jennifer made it sound so simple. Just like ABC.

"How do I do that?"

"Find his weakness, set a trap, and then go out and get him." There it was. The secret to Jennifer's success. And Emily didn't know any more about how to do it than she had before she'd asked.

"He doesn't have any weaknesses," she said, dejected. She popped the last of the cocoa-coated banana into her mouth and rose from her chair to throw away the peel. "He's perfect."

"Emily. Emily." Jennifer's despair for poor Emily rang throughout the room. "Everyone has a weakness. There are very few of us who are perfect." She tried to look humble, and when she got tired of that, she added, "But you're a smart girl, and you'll find this man's vulnerable spot. And if you want him bad enough, you'll think of some clever way to get him."

What do I do then? was Emily's next question, but she thought it prudent to keep it to herself. Jennifer had a way of making the most simple things sound complicated . . . and vice versa.

Wednesdays and weekends were usually long and uneventful for Emily. Those were the days she didn't go in to work. If she could have had her way, the center would have been open seven days a week, and she would have gone in for six of them. As it was, she could get funding for only four days, and she'd cut back on her own salary to keep an assistant and pay her a fair wage. Thankfully Emily led a quiet life and didn't have to pay rent.

This particular Sunday seemed duller than most. With Jennifer gone by noon, she rattled around alone in the old tomb of a house she called home. Built in the late 1800s, the house was set on a shale foundation and made of stones. There were huge columns along the veranda that embraced the house on three sides. The house looked much the same as it always had. The trim was white, and perennials grew profusely along the circular drive.

Inside, the rooms were big and situated in the prescribed order of the era—formal rooms in front and the domestic area in the rear of the house. Emily had always thought this arrangement a little stupid, as the morning sunshine came in through the front windows, which meant the kitchen was sweltering in the afternoon. Emily could remember having many summer salads for supper in her youth. Her mother had hated cooking in the heat.

The house had been tended to with love. Each generation had cared for the wood trim, papered and painted the walls, fixed the plumbing, and mended the holes in the roof. And Emily would do the same now that it was her responsibility. There were days, however, when the thought of working on the house for the rest of her life gave way to the idea of donating the place to the college as a museum or sorority house or something.

Emily sighed and flopped down into the chair behind the big oak desk in her father's old study. She knew she'd never give the house away. She'd lumber along under the burden passed on to her by her parents because it was her duty. And everyone knew that good ol' Emily never shirked her duty, never failed to be there when needed, never rocked the boat. The more she thought about it, the madder she got. She was tired of being good ol' Emily.

Bang, bang, bang. Three times she thumped her fist down on her father's desk in anger and frustration. ABC. "Weakness, trap, go get him." The words echoed through her mind as they would through the house if she'd spoken them out loud.

"Weakness, trap, go get him." It sounded so easy. It also sounded cold and calculating, which wasn't a mode Emily normally operated in. Then again, that was probably the reason people thought of her as poor Emily, she decided in disgust. Poor sweet, loyal, innocent, unassuming, undemanding, easy-to-get-along-with Emily. Oh, no one had ever come right out and called her that to her face. But it was there in their voices more often than she cared to remember. She was thirty years old, and she wasn't a threat to anyone. She was just a horribly nice person doing everything people expected of her and stuck with an albatross of a house with no husband or children to live in it with her. That wasn't a life. That was an existence. And Emily knew she wanted more. She had more to give. She wanted to live before she was too old to enjoy it. Jennifer was right. She *needed* a life!

Jennifer had a life. She knew how to go out and get what she wanted. Emily knew how to get what she wanted too. Only she never seemed to be asking for something for herself. She worked like crazy getting funding and donations for the center and the college. She talked a nurse into donating one afternoon a month to check blood pressures. She raised money for portable keyboards. In college she once coerced a teacher into giving a pregnant, overstressed friend a second chance on a final exam. And she'd even found a job for a young, unemployed mechanic, one of her less strange dates, as she recalled.

Maybe it was time to ask for something for herself, to get something for herself. Maybe it was time to kill poor Emily and start being cold and calculating.

She opened the drawer of the desk and took out paper and a pencil. Okay, she thought, ABC. Weakness, trap, go get him.

Weaknesses, weaknesses, her mind scanned the subject as objectively as possible. His face and body were perfect. He was intelligent, witty, and very kind to have put up with her all evening. No, his weakness wasn't obvious.

Drugs, women, alcohol? No, it would have to be something more simple. Money? He was a lawyer from an old family and most likely was loaded. Career? He could probably pick and choose jobs and was exactly where he wanted to be. What else was there? She racked her brain and chewed on the end of her pencil until . . .

Ego. He was confident of himself, but he'd been a little touchy about that disgraced old ancestor of his. He'd all but accused William Joseph of having the money his great-great-grandfather was court-martialed for losing. Lost? Ha. A likely story. But it was the only vulnerable spot she'd seen in him in their short acquaintance. If she could think of some sort of trap to set, she might get to know him well enough to find another, better weakness. This one would have to do for now.

She picked up the phone and immediately started to dial. A letter would take too long. So would walking out into the hall to get the professor's letter which had his phone number inscribed at the bottom. The dean of students would know how to get hold of the professor.

"Odd fellow, that one," Dean Windtharp commented absently. Emily could hear him shuffling through papers, looking for Professor McEntire's number. "Did he tell you his family owns one of the oldest and largest law firms in Philadelphia?"

"No. He didn't." Lawyer, old family, old family law firm. She was glad she hadn't spent too much time looking for a weakness there.

"Everyone assumed he'd go into the firm and make up for his older brother's desertion to the public defender's office. He graduated fourth in his class at Harvard, and then do you know what he did?"

"Decided to teach business law at Princeton?"

"Well, he did that, too, which upset his family, but before that he went to work with his brother in the P.D.'s office. For the experience, he'd told them. They almost disowned him then, but he didn't fall into complete disgrace until he opened his legal aid clinic."

"Did they disown him?" she asked, feeling an instant anger toward the professor's self-righteous family.

"Oh, no, no," he assured her. "They're just not very happy with him at the moment. They're still hoping he'll come to his senses." The dean's tone told her that he, too, thought Professor McEntire was missing a few pages of the program. Emily, however, liked the idea of him taking his own path in the world. It went very nicely with her image of him being a one-of-a-kind sort of man.

She wrote down the number as the dean gave it to her, thanked him, hung up, and immediately dialed the professor. The phone rang four times, and she was about to hang up when the deep, intimate male voice of her dreams answered. It was as breathless as she felt. She tried to match her rapid respirations to his panting.

"Hello? Is anyone there?" he asked.

"Oh. Hello. Professor McEntire? This is Emily Becket. Have I caught you at a bad time? You sound a little winded."

"Emily." She loved it when he called her that. "I was just thinking about you."

"You were?"

"Uh-huh. I was out jogging. I ran past your house and . . ."

"You did?" She swiveled in her chair to look out the front window, as if she could still catch sight of his dust.

"I was going to stop by," he went on to say, "but then I thought maybe I ought to call first." He paused briefly. "I'm glad you called."

"Why?"

There was another short silence before he answered. "Because it means you want to talk to me again."

Well, why wouldn't she want to talk to him again? He was the most exciting thing ever to happen in her life. She wanted to know all there was to know about him. She wanted to share her tiny, innermost dreams with him. She wanted him to like her, care about her. Why wouldn't she want to talk to him again?

"Emily?"

"Yes?"

"Was there something special you wanted to talk about? Or . . . did you just want to talk."

"Ah. No. I had a specific reason." It's now or never, Emily, she told herself. She took a deep, shuddering breath. "I've been giving some thought to your taking a look at my great-great-grandfather's papers. At the risk of repeating myself, I have to tell you again that they're extremely boring, and you won't discover any fabulous Civil War secrets in them. But if it will help settle things in your mind about your own relative, I think you should look at them."

"Are you sure you don't mind? I don't want to intrude on your privacy just to satisfy my curiosity. It isn't that big a deal." He was being very considerate, but Emily could hear the eagerness in his voice. He'd taken the bait.

"Not at all. I just hope you don't have an allergy to dust."

"I don't. When would be a good time to start?"

"I'm off all day Wednesday, if that's a good day for you."

"It's fine. But . . ." He left his objection hanging on a note of blighted hope.

"But what?"

"Well, I was hoping I'd be able to see you sooner than that. Would you consider going out to dinner with me on Monday or Tuesday or even tonight?" Cold and calculating was paying off. Why hadn't she listened to Jennifer before now?

She would have sold her soul to accept his invitation, but a good trap was going to take some time. She had the rest of the day and two evenings after work in which to figure something out. Anticipating an evening out with him would

drive her nuts and distract her from her goal.
Besides, if things went well . . .

"I'd really love to, but things are a little hectic
for me right now. We're planning a concert in the
park for next weekend, and rehearsals have been
running a little late. It's our first public perfor-
mance, and everyone's a little nervous."

"These are folks from the center you're talking
about," he said, but it was more of a question
than a statement.

"Yes. And stage fright aside, I think they're going
to be wonderful."

"You already think they're pretty wonderful, don't
you? The people, I mean. You're very fond of the
elderly people you work with. I can tell by the way
you talk about them."

A little friendly manipulation was one thing,
but lying was something else. She didn't care if
Jennifer thought her work boring, she wouldn't
lie about something so close to her heart.

"I am. They're terrific people, and there ain't a
throwaway in the bunch, to quote Bernie."

"Bernie?"

"One of my favorites."

"I see. Well, then, I guess Wednesday is the
day." Emily thought he was about to say more,
but the line remained quiet.

"Fine. I'll see you then—then," she stammered
awkwardly, reluctant to end the conversation.

"Okay. And, Emily?"

"Yes?"

"Thank you."

"You're welcome."

Five

Setting traps wasn't something Emily did on a routine basis. As a matter of fact, she'd never *ever* set one for a man before. This wasn't the first time she'd heard of the procedure, of course. She'd heard it talked about quite often. But it had always sounded sneaky and underhanded and not like something she'd want to do to someone.

However, by the time Emily settled on her plan of action, she had fairly well come to the conclusion that not all traps had to be devious or dishonest. A trap could also be a slight stretching of the truth or a mere slowing down of an inevitable conclusion to a particular event. She wasn't going to have to break the jogger's leg to get him to slow down long enough to notice her, and she was considerably relieved.

Since the bait was to be the stack of old papers in the attic, Emily felt the trap would have to involve them as well. She'd spent that entire Sunday afternoon, after speaking with Professor McEntire on the phone, reexamining her great-great-grandfather's logs. They certainly hadn't gotten any juicier over the years. They were as boring and dry as they had been when she and Jennifer read them as teenagers.

Ordinarily a couple of boy-crazy teenagers wouldn't have wasted several days rummaging through an old farmer's personal notes. That she and her cousin had involved a long story that centered around their discovery of an old well under the gazebo in the backyard. . . .

"The next time you throw your diary under here, Jenny, you're going to have to either leave it there or come after it yourself, because *I'm* not crawling under here ever again," Emily could remember saying. Clearer than her words, she could remember the cold, damp mud that squished through her fingers and clung to her bare knees as she searched in the darkness for her cousin's diary. "And don't tell me there aren't any bugs under here, 'cuz I can feel 'em watching me."

"Just get it," Jennifer said, very much put out. "And stop calling me Jenny. I told you before that I only meant to set it inside here. But you scared me when you came out, and I pitched it too far. That makes it as much your fault as it is mine. So stop complaining."

"And I told you that my mother would never read your dumb old diary. You should put it under your mattress like I do mine."

"Well, if you didn't tell her, and she didn't read my diary, how did she know when I got my period?" Jennifer asked, confident that she had the ultimate proof of her aunt's spying.

"Mothers just know that kind of stuff. I'll bet your mother knows, and she hasn't been here in months," Emily said. It was meant to be a comforting remark, but looking back, it had probably hurt Jennifer to be reminded of her mother's long absences.

Something hard and angular met her finger-tips, but it wasn't the diary. "Shine the light over here a little more, Jennifer. I've found something."

The low light showed pieces of board nailed into the shape of a square, lying flat on the ground. It didn't look particularly important at first, but when she caught sight of the diary on the far side of the board and reached over to pick it up, she felt a swish of cold air rise up through the boards and cool her warm cheeks.

"It's a hole. A deep one. What do you think it is?"

"How should I know? And now ask me if I care." Jennifer had always been glib.

Emily picked up a small pebble and dropped it through a slit in the boards. Either the pebble wasn't big enough to make a clear sound when it hit bottom, or the hole was endless, because she didn't hear it land. "It might be an old well. Daddy says there's a couple of them hereabouts, but that they were probably filled in or overgrown by now."

"So?"

"So," she said, grabbing the diary and wiggling out of the crawl space beneath the gazebo. "They say ol' William Joseph hid a fortune of money in his well once for the army."

"What army?"

"The Confederate army, stupid. You remember the Civil War, don't you?" Jennifer glared at her. "Well, what if that's the well? What if the treasure is still there? What if it's been sitting down there all this time, and I discovered it."

"Oh. Good, Emily. You mean to tell me you actually think that if there was a fortune buried under your gazebo, your family would still be poor? My mother says your father is like a dog with a new bone when it comes to money. He'd have sniffed it out before now, don't you think?"

"Maybe he doesn't know the well's there."

"Maybe he does and knows that it's empty."

Well, one thing had led to another, and Emily had finally won out—or at least she'd convinced Jennifer to stay in the attic with her while she tried to find some information about the well. She'd been profoundly disappointed to discover it clearly marked on some old maps and described as a dry hole. And the only mention made of a well in William Joseph's papers had been a line noting a night when "some of Lee's boys stopped to use the well." Presumably the one they'd used had had water in it.

The door chimes rang and jingled disjointedly through Emily's memories of the past.

This was it, then. The bait was laid. The trap was set. And the professor was at the door. She stood and smoothed out the nonexistent wrinkles in her full floral-print skirt, patted her yellow cotton sweater into place, and took a huge breath that did nothing to dispel the qualms she had about carrying out her plan.

And she did have her misgivings. A trap was a trap, after all. No matter how she'd chosen to define it or cover it up with fancy excuses and explanations, it would always be plain old trickery. And trickery wasn't normally Emily's style.

"Too late now," she said aloud, wondering where the courage and aplomb she'd used to practice this scene had gone. She tried to focus her attention on the drumming sound of the spring rain as the drops splattered against the windowpanes. She made herself walk slowly to the door, but her heart beat her there by ten paces when she saw the shadow of a very familiar body through the frosted glass.

"Good morning, Professor McEntire," she said, mentally patting herself on the back for sounding calmer than she felt.

"Good morning, Emily. It's good to see you again." His voice was the sexiest thing she'd ever heard. Which was very disconcerting at times, as it made everything he said seem intimate and provocative.

"Please come in." Said the spider to the fly, she added for her own benefit. Looking into those deep, thoughtful eyes brought on a fresh, new supply of guilt, and Emily had to quickly review her motives for deceiving him.

"Thank you," he said, shaking the rain from his hair and leather jacket before stepping inside.

That body of his seemed to bring the old house to life. He didn't look weak or puny in proportion to the high ceilings. The walls sort of closed in around him and fit him perfectly. Emily was growing accustomed to the fact that what seemed drab and dreary to her in an everyday way actually took on Technicolor at the very thought of him. It only made sense that the house should seem vivid when he came to call.

They stood, very ill at ease with each other, for several moments before Emily thought to speak again. "Well, this is it, Professor McEntire. Welcome to Becket House," she said, turning to lead the way to the front parlor. "Please feel free to make yourself comfortable here. We've had Yankees visit before, and the house seems to tolerate it quite well."

He laughed. "That's good to know. And it's Noble."

Emily looked around the old room at the fine antiques and family portraits with a considering eye. "Well, it is very old and it does have a certain charm about it. And there's certainly been a lot of Becket history made here. But I don't think I'd go so far as to call it noble. There were other houses built about the same time, some earlier, that are much nicer than this one. In fact, have you been to—"

"No," he broke in, carefully drawing her full attention back to him. "What I meant was that my name is Noble. I'd like you to call me by my given name."

"Oh. I'm sorry. What a weird name. Well, not weird. Unusual, I guess is better," she stammered, tripping over her own tongue once again and feeling like a fool. After all, what other name could his mother have given him that suited as well? "Is it a family name?"

"As a matter of fact, it is. Remember the lieutenant in the Union army I was telling you about?" Emily nodded. "He was the first Noble McEntire."

"Ah. And so the interest to clear the name," she concluded sagely, leading the way to the front parlor. "Would you like some coffee before I take you up? Or would you like to take some with you and get right to work on this crusade of yours to exonerate your namesake."

"I see you still think your great-great-grandfather was totally innocent in this affair," he said with humor rather than malice. He set his briefcase down beside a floral-print Queen Anne chair and sat down.

"Gracious, no. From all I've heard, he was a very wily old fellow. I'm sure his innocence lasted only until he reached the age of reason. But to answer your question, I do still feel that if he ever had the money, there would be a record of it. And there isn't. Do you take anything in your coffee?" she asked as she filled two cups from the carafe she'd set out.

"No. And you don't think he could have hidden it for a time and then given it back to the Confederates who originally stole it?" He took the ceramic mug from Emily's hand, and of course their fingers touched lightly, just as she'd hoped they would. He had big hands with long, graceful fingers that were fascinating to watch—and even more fascinating to be touched by.

"Ah, no." She had to recall the question. "The War Between the States has been researched and written about so often that if a large sum of money had mysteriously cropped up in the middle of it, someone would have noticed, and then it would have been researched and written about all over again. Eventually they would have figured out where it came from, and your great-great-grandfather would have been cleared. Right?"

"It would seem so. But then that brings us back to the original problem. And I've been doing some interesting research of my own lately, which would lead me to believe that the rumor about your great-great-grandfather isn't so far off base."

For all his perfection, this noble Noble McEntire had one huge flaw which had the uncanny ability to rub Emily the wrong way. He seemed determined to besmirch her family name. The task would prove to be impossible, she knew, but his intention was irksome nonetheless.

"Well, you're certainly welcome to try to prove your theory, but I'm afraid you're going to be sadly disappointed," she said, playing her part easily because it was the one she always played. And she had to admit, as far as her little scheme was concerned, his interest in her family served her purpose very well—almost too well in that she found it so annoying. "If you're ready, I'll take you upstairs so you can get started."

The attic was a huge room crammed with several lifetimes of memorabilia. Years ago, when it had become apparent that a steady stream of investigators would be passing time there—and passing out during the hot summer months—a desk and an exhaust fan had been installed for their comfort. Emily's grandmother, her father's mother, had been a fastidious person who felt compelled to put in shelves and to store and label all those years of Becket debris. Emily's mother, on the other hand, had been tidy but not compulsively clean, and during her reign the junk had dribbled out onto the floor again so that the attic now looked as it should but in an uncommonly organized way.

Emily had left the fan running through the night, but nothing could remove the old musty odor that clung to everything in the room. She'd brought up the airtight metal boxes that held William Joseph's papers from her own study the day before. They now stood in readiness on the desk for Noble McEntire.

"I'll leave you to it, then," she said once he was comfortable. "If you have any questions . . ."

"You're not leaving, are you?" he asked, bewildered. He quickly reached inside his briefcase and pulled out a thick packet of papers. "I brought some of my own research with me. I . . . I thought you might like to read the other side's story. Maybe take a look at the puzzle from a different perspective."

She smiled at him smugly and cocked her head to one side. "What puzzle? I told you before that the whole thing is nonsense. Rumors."

"Please. Stay. Read what I've brought you. At least then you'll understand why I think of it as a puzzle."

Sitting within viewing distance of him and reading his notes on the Civil War would certainly beat pacing around on the first floor waiting for him to have a question, she decided pragmatically.

"Okay. But you have to promise that you won't hold it against me if I start to snore," she said sprightly. "In fact, I think I'd better go down and bring up my coffee. If this material of yours is anything like my great-great-grandfather's, I'm going to need it."

She ran both ways and was breathless when she returned to the attic with her cup, the coffeepot, and a box of chewy caramel cookies. "Midmorning munchies," she said with a shrug as Noble took in her armload of supplies. Too late, she remembered that health-oriented people would rather die than get a good sugar buzz. She sighed, deciding that he may as well know just how imperfect she was, right off the bat. Flaws, like her weakness for sweets, couldn't be hidden forever.

He had moved an old wing chair to one side of the desk and positioned it to face his chair. The situation suited Emily fine, and she would have taken it to heart except that she realized that it was also the best arrangement for sharing the lamplight. She would have gone blind trying to read using only the overhead light.

She set the coffeepot and box of cookies on the desk between them and got comfortable in the chair. Then, with all the courage she could muster, she put on her reading glasses. Oh, she knew it was vain and stupid to care what he thought about her having to wear glasses to read, but she did. She wanted him to think she was as perfect as a woman could be. She wanted him to think she was a flawless creature who never made mistakes and was incredibly beautiful and charming.

But the truth was, she was just Emily. Bait and trap notwithstanding, it was still Emily who would have to "go get him."

"This better be good, Professor. I'm going to take some convincing, you know," she said, deciding to pretend she wasn't wearing the glasses in the hope that he might not notice them.

"Everything here can be substantiated," he said, handing her the packet with a casual glance. He scooted his chair closer to the desk and shuffled papers, preparing to get down to business. "We were a little better organized during the war and kept better records."

"Oh? *Did* you?" Emily raised her brow at the hint of challenge in his voice.

"Yes, *we* did," he stated, grinning as he popped on a pair of dark-rimmed glasses.

"Ah. I take it we're at war, then, Professor?" she said, taking up his dare, warming instantly to the sight of him in glasses.

"Only until you see things my way, Miss Becket. Then we can call a truce."

North against South. Man against woman. Emily was beginning to understand why Jennifer liked to play these games. "What happens when you find out how wrong your thinking is, Yank?"

"Then I'll surrender unconditionally." Emily liked the sound of that. Dreams were spun from such words. She smiled at him in premature triumph and turned her attention to the papers in her lap. The sooner the trap snapped, and he raised his white flag, the better she'd like it.

Reading had never been a chore for Emily, but even simulating being deeply engrossed in the heavily fact-laden material Noble had given her was more than she could handle. She tried. She even found it slightly interesting. But it wasn't as captivating as watching Noble while he pored over her great-great-grandfather's papers.

Time and again she would finish reading a paragraph, only to realize that she hadn't understood a word of it. She'd reread it and then finally give up and go back to watching Noble, keeping her head bent and her lids at half mast.

It was very strange, she thought, the way he looked so . . . human sometimes. Sitting there watching him chew on caramel cookies, his chin propped on his fist, Emily had the sensation that he was like a mythical god come to life. He didn't look so far away and unattainable anymore. It was as if he'd stepped down off the pedestal she'd put him on and become a living, breathing mortal.

His downcast eyes and the spread of his eyelashes across his cheeks made him look very vulnerable and capable of being hurt. There were tiny creases between his brows that led her to believe he had worries and concerns, that he'd been confused and disappointed just like everybody else. Even the lines around his mouth seemed to tell her that he was acquainted with pain and sorrow, and something deep inside her stirred and reached out to him. It was something nonsexual, dynamically potent, and too complicated to explain. Emily shuddered in its aftermath and felt an odd sort of mixture of fear and joy settle in her chest.

Noble reached out blindly for the box of cookies, shook it, and then peered into its empty depths before glancing over at Emily.

"I ate all your munchies," he said in a way that must have endeared him greatly to his mother.

"It's after noon. You were probably starving," she said, smiling, wondering what her chances were of seducing a sugar-intoxicated jock.

He shook his head and grinned at her sheep-ishly. "Bad habit. I'm a snacker from way back. I fight a constant battle with my weight."

"You do?"

"Mmm. When I was a kid, I was as big as a barn. Now I run."

"Really? You were fat?" Somehow it seemed inconceivable that his body was ever anything but perfect.

He nodded. "I lived a teenager's nightmare. I didn't discover exercise until I was in college. I roomed with this hockey jock who hated my guts because I was all brains and blubber. Eventually we became friends. I taught him Latin and calculus, and he taught me how to run." He gave a short laugh in recollection. "Actually he taught me how to run before we became friends. He used to chase me around campus on a motorcycle."

"Why?" she asked, horrified, empathizing with the overweight young man he had once been.

"Just to be mean, I guess."

"Well, how did you become friends, then?"

"I got sick of it and finally took a swing at him. We had this huge fight in our dorm room, broke a window and a desk, destroyed the place. Anyway, I eventually fell on him and broke his arm." He laughed. "He couldn't play hockey for the rest of the season and started running to stay in shape for the next year. I asked if I could run with him. . . . I felt a little guilty and I wanted to make up with him somehow. He finally said I could if I helped him with his studies."

"Well, that was big of him." Emily couldn't believe that young man's gall.

Noble laughed. "We're still good friends, and he's still incredibly cocky. Thinks he owns the whole world." He stood and stretched his aching back muscles. Then he sat on the top of the desk next to Emily, saying, "I really envy him sometimes."

"Why?" she asked automatically, wanting to know all there was to know about him. His thoughts, his dreams, his opinions. Why he'd envy an arrogant jerk of a hockey player when he gave every impression of having everything together in the first place.

"Because I think it would be nice to have all that confidence in yourself. To make a decision and assume it's the right one. To make demands of the world and assume that you'll get what you want. To be bold enough to simply take what you want out of life."

Emily was fascinated. She leaned forward in her chair and asked, "What is it you want? What don't you feel bold enough to reach out and take?"

Although he normally looked her straight in the eye when he spoke to her, he now lowered his lids as if trying to hide his thoughts. For long moments the only sound to be heard was the pelting of the rain on the roof. When at last his head came up, his gaze was deliberate and reflective, warm and abysmal.

"You," he said simply.

"What?" Her voice cracked as his answer bounced off the attic walls, vibrating Emily's whole world out of focus. Her body throbbed with the pounding of her heart. She tried to swallow the thickness in her throat, but it held firm.

"You see, if I were my friend and I wanted to kiss you, I'd put my hand out like this and just assume that you'd take it."

"You would?" Automatically she laid her hand in his. She felt a shiver of excitement pass through her, all the way down to her toes, as his fingers closed gently around hers.

"Ah-ha. Then I'd take it one step further," he said, guiding her to her feet to stand before him. "By assuming that you want this kiss as much as I do."

"I do—I see," she stammered, watching his eyes as they grew serious with desire and passion, glancing at his mouth as it came closer to hers. Her breath caught and held in her lungs when the palm of his hand brushed across her cheek and his fingers moved into her hair. She suffered the most ungodly feeling that she might explode before his lips finally came to rest on hers.

A series of tender, sipping kisses and a tug on her bottom lip turned everything inside her to a quivering, gelatinous mass of yearning. She put her arms around his neck and touched the soft curls along the nape of his neck, which apparently led him to assume that it was time to deepen his kisses as his tongue slipped between her lips. He wrapped his arms about her, pulling her closer as he explored the sensitive spots in her mouth, tickling her tongue with his.

Emily instinctively pressed nearer, insinuating herself between his legs, all too aware of his maleness as her pelvis leaned into and cradled the evidence of his arousal. He groaned, and through the muddle in her mind she could feel his hands burning, testing, and exploring her body. Intuitively, he seemed to know where she was most vulnerable to his touch. It was as if they'd made love to each other before, and he knew exactly what pleased and incited her.

Her senses reeled, careening through a space and time she'd never known before. His fingers found bare skin under her sweater. He ignited her nerve endings, setting off a chain of convulsive explosions that nearly drove her out of her mind with passion. Her soft, silky camisole was no defense against his searching hands. His hand found her breasts and pressed a hardened tip deep into his palm.

She gasped for air, breaking off the kiss, arching against the source of her pleasure. She felt the finely tuned muscles taut and shivering under her fingertips. She felt the control and the power in his body as he trailed hot, searing kisses down her neck. A gray hazy fog clouded her vision, so she kept her eyes closed. With nothing else to focus on, her body and mind were incapable of discerning and responding to anything but the ecstasy he was creating with his hands and lips.

Suddenly his mouth was at her breast. Her hand slid into his dark wavy hair, and she held him close as he tugged gently and drew her into a state of pleasure that made her weak with a need for more.

Her knees buckled under her, and that panicky feeling of falling shattered the spell and brought Emily upright into reality.

"Ah . . ." Her breath squeaked through her vocal cords, sounding weak and unstable. "I'll bet you're starving. I was just going to go down to make us some lunch. I know I'm hungry," she babbled, stepping away from him as she righted her sweater. "Oh. Will you look at that! It's nearly two-thirty. I'm definitely hungry . . . for some food. How about you? Are you hungry?"

When she could finally trust herself to look at him without turning into a lump of goo inside, she discovered he had the sweetest, most tender, most knowing expression on his face that she had ever seen. She saw his own awe and wonder at what had just passed between them and his

understanding that it was as potentially dangerous as it was enlivening.

"I'm always hungry. Can I help?" he asked, pushing himself away from the desk and walking toward
her.

"No. Oh, no," she said, holding her hands out
in front of her protectively. "You finish reading
those farm reports over there, and I'll be back in a
jiffy. No trouble. Nothing fancy. Just lunch."

She left him standing in the middle of the attic
with his hands in his pockets, watching her make
a fool of herself. By the time she reached the first
floor, she'd come to some very firm conclusions
about Noble McEntire. If that man was lacking
the confidence to reach out and grab what he
wanted from life, then her name wasn't Emily
Becket.

Six

As promised, Emily returned to the attic a short while later, which was actually quite a feat in itself, as she couldn't remember what she'd gone to the kitchen for in the first place. She'd sat at the kitchen table for some time, staring into space and wondering if she might not have gnawed off more than she could chew. Noble McEntire was no amateur kisser.

All her best instincts told her to forget the trap, let him read William Joseph's papers, and let him go. Noble was as quiet and majestic as any snowcapped mountain she'd ever seen. But under all that splendor and gentleness was an active volcano that could change her life so completely, she might not recognize it. She had the distinct impression that she was playing with fire—and still it tempted her.

In a daze she loaded a picnic basket with sandwiches, cheese, fruit, wine, and whatever else she came across to distract him with. She needed time to rethink the situation.

If he could kiss that passionately, he might be

just as passionate about being duped into hunting for a treasure that never existed. All she'd ever wanted was more time with him. But at the rate things were going, time didn't seem to matter. What mattered most was the quality of the time not the quantity. Trickery didn't have much of a quality ring to it, and more and more it grated on her conscience.

"I was beginning to think you'd been wounded in action down there," he said even before she'd topped the stairs and come into his view.

Her heart sank with dismay when she looked across the room at him, only to find him just as incredibly handsome and desirable as he had been when she'd left. Her stomach tied itself in knots, and her heart rate began to pick up speed.

"I was shooting truth serum through the cork in the wine bottle with a syringe. Counterespionage is a Becket specialty," she said, falling back into her role, eager to keep the conversation light and whimsical. "I'm planning to ply you with wine, and wheedle all your secrets from you."

He left the desk and was walking toward her, shaking his head in disapproval. "That kind of trickery is beneath you, Emily. All the really beautiful spies use a gentler, more intimate method of gathering information, which is far more effective." He gave the picnic basket some consideration, then looked back at Emily with a wily smirk on his face. "That was your plan all along, wasn't it? You were lying about the wine just to throw me off, weren't you? You planned a romantic little picnic here in the attic to seduce me and win from me all the secrets I hold in my heart. Isn't that right?"

Emily was so confused, she didn't know what to react to first. His use of the words *trickery* and *lying.* His calling her beautiful. The rather pointed innuendo that they were about to have more than lunch on the blanket she'd brought up for their picnic. Or the half-teasing, half-serious look in his eyes that made her want to giggle and faint dead away at the same time.

Suddenly, from out of the chaos in her mind, a very Jennifer-like notion came to her. When in doubt, attack. "My word, you Yankee men *are* sharp. It's no wonder you won the war. But don't think I'm giving up just because you've found me out."

"Forewarned is forearmed, Miss Emily. And I don't plan to be the second McEntire duped by a southerner. Test me, torture me, tempt me with your beauty. My lips are sealed," he said, obviously liking her spunk, warming to their imaginary battle.

He took the blanket, and after looking around for a good spot, spread it out under one of the tall windows at the end of the house. He walked off in another direction and returned momentarily with two candles and a box of stick matches. With the rain blurring the windows and holding back what dreary light there was from outdoors, the candle glowed romantically in that one little corner of the attic.

She heard herself swallow hard as she watched him light the second candle and then turn to her expectantly. She wanted to saunter over and act calm and sophisticated, as if this happened every day. But she felt nailed to the floor, the pulse in her throat nearly choking her.

Noble, however, didn't appear to have a nerve in his body when he came to her, pried the basket out of her fingers, and helped her across the room to the blanket. He sat down close beside her.

"I had a chance to look around a little while you were downstairs. You've got some great stuff up here. Did you ever come up on rainy days when you were a kid and play dress-up?" he asked as if she weren't acting like a zombie.

She nodded, and her hands automatically began to set out lunch as she spoke. "Jennifer and I used to come up here and play for hours on end. The best thing was, we could pick almost any era we wanted. Sometimes we were belles, sometimes flappers, sometimes we wore fancy hats and bustles. It would all depend on what kind of mood we were in. And sometimes, when Jennifer wanted to get all dolled up and go to a fancy ball, I'd dress up with a cape and a top hat, and we'd dance until dinnertime," she said, laughing softly at her fond recollections.

"What about when you wanted to go to the ball? Did Jennifer take the man's role?" Noble asked, choosing a sandwich and taking a bite as carefully as he'd asked the question.

"Well, my hair was always very curly, and my mother kept it short so we could control it." She sighed involuntarily. "Jennifer always had long, beautiful dark hair that she could put pretty combs and pins into. It just sort of made sense that she should be the girl on those occasions. Why do you ask?"

He shrugged. "I was just wondering."

"Don't you like Jennifer?" she asked, responding to something negative in his voice.

"No. No. It isn't that I don't like her. I hardly know her. She's just . . . not like you, that's all."

"Of course she's not like me. What does that mean?"

"Nothing, really, I guess. It's just that women like your cousin scare me to death. I've always had the feeling they could chew a man up and spit him out without batting an eye. I was just wondering if she'd always had . . . a strong personality."

As much as she loved Jennifer, there was a heavy element of truth in Noble's observation, and she couldn't hold it against him. But she could try to make him understand.

Her father and Jennifer's mother had been brother and sister, Emily explained. Jennifer's mother, who was considerably older, had married well. Her husband had invested her share of what had once been the Becket fortune soundly, so that Jennifer was fairly well funded, although not stinking rich as she wanted to be. Emily's father, on the other hand, had lost most of what was his in the stock market crash of 1929, not through any fault of his own but because he was still young and his money was tied up with his father's, who also lost heavily that year.

Jennifer's parents had little time for either the poor relatives or the daughter born late in their lives. Jennifer came to live at Becket House during her school vacations and on holidays. And even though it was extremely obvious right from the start that Jennifer and Emily had nothing in common, they formed a tight, lasting bond over the years through patience, endurance, and understanding.

"Jennifer has always been a little spoiled and outspoken, but she's not had the nicest life either. Her parents all but ignored her, and she's been married several times. She's developed this crusty exterior, which is all most people see. But deep inside she's very soft and vulnerable. And I love her very much."

"I can see that, and I envy her," he said, his

eyes warm and tender as he regarded her intently. "Tell me about your life. What was it like? Why are you so special, so sweet and loving and gentle?"

She lowered her gaze from his, feeling self-conscious but liking it very much that he thought she was all those things. She'd never considered herself particularly sweet or gentle; then again, she'd never given it much thought. She'd always been simply Emily. What she did, the way she felt, and how she acted was all natural. It was just the way she was and always had been. She'd never thought of herself as being anything but ordinary. That Noble thought she was special thrilled her beyond belief.

"I think I had a very normal life growing up," she said in a soft voice, unsure of what he wanted to hear. "We weren't wealthy, like Jennifer's parents, but I always had everything I ever wanted. My father was a professor over at the college. And my mother was active in the church and in the community. She was always doing nice things for other people. . . ."

Emily went on to tell of a happy childhood and vacation trips with her parents and cousin. College and her career were next on the list, and Noble listened attentively, asking questions that took her down other avenues of her past.

It was over a very juicy orange that she told him about the senior citizens' center and how much the people had come to mean to her.

"I truly can't understand how our society can ignore its elderly. They're so full of life for today, and they have such wonderful stories of yesterday, and . . . and they're so grateful for every tomorrow that comes their way. And they're smart." She popped another orange section into her mouth, the juice running down into the palm of her hand. She'd long ago forgotten how nervous Noble made her and was talking as if she'd always known him. "This Bernie, the one I told you about the other day? Well, he didn't finish high school, but he's always been an avid reader, and the things he knows just amaze me. And he's very wise. About life, you know? It seems such a shame that when he dies, all that knowledge and wisdom will go with him. It's too bad there isn't some way he could leave it behind or pass it on to someone else."

"Like you, for instance?" he asked, smiling at her.

"I'd love to know all the things Bernie knows," she said with great respect.

"I have a hunch you will someday."

"I hope so. It definitely would be something to look forward to in my old age," she said, reaching for a napkin to wipe the sticky juice from her fingers. When Noble caught her hand, she was surprised. When he turned it palm-up and tested the stickiness with his tongue, she was perplexed. When he gently licked the tip of each finger, her mind shut down and her sensory system took over.

"Know what I'm looking forward to right now?" he asked, watching her expression closely as he slipped her index finger into his mouth and slowly sucked the juice off.

"Dessert?" she asked, finding it hard to speak around the huge lump in her throat.

"Better than dessert," he said, moving on to her middle finger. Little chills marched up her arm. The muscle in her abdomen coiled excitedly, and she began to throb deep down inside. "I'm waiting for that seduction you promised me. I can't wait to see which one of us weakens first and starts blabbing secrets."

"Oh, but I don't have any secrets," she said shakily as his tongue wrapped itself around her little finger, and the tips of her breasts began to tingle.

"Sure you do. So do I. We share a special secret that's never been spoken before." He teased the palm of her hand with his tongue, licking away the orange juice, dissolving Emily's willpower as he went along. With his other hand he removed the basket, which was now filled with trash, from between them.

"We do?" Her arm was beginning to tremble under the onslaught of sensations it was enduring. The rest of her body was screaming in impatience, waiting for its share of Noble's exquisite attentions.

"It's the secret I discovered the first time I saw you, in the hardware store. The one you already knew when we met in the graveyard that day," he said, folding her juice-free hand in his and leaning closer so that his lips were mere inches from hers. "Our bodies know the secret, don't they, Emily?"

Mesmerized by the depth and the passion in his eyes, Emily could manage only a singular nod of her head before his mouth covered hers. If the secret was that she wanted him more than she'd ever wanted anything or anyone in her entire life, then her heart, soul, *and* body knew it and rejoiced in it.

She opened herself to him completely, slipping quickly from the world she knew into a place where only she and Noble existed. Their tongues met and teased, their breath mingled and became as one. Her hands reached out toward the body that had first attracted her; she touched the man, and unveiled a predestined bond between them. It was a linking of their souls that was so strong, so powerful and deep, it seemed timeless, as if it had always been there and always would be.

They came together like two perfect pieces of a puzzle. Her body soft and fluid, his strong and solid. With one hand against the braided hair at the back of her head, he held her close while his other hand trailed down her arm to her hip and along her thigh.

She felt tremors of pent-up emotions in the muscles of his back and shoulders. She longed to touch the healthy, glowing skin her mind could recall all too easily. Remembering all the hours she'd spent daydreaming about the feel and texture of it beneath her fingertips was almost more than she could bear. Boldly her hands moved under his sweater to pull the tail of his shirt from his pants.

He drew in a deep, audible breath when she touched his bare skin. With this first taste of pleasure, her hunger grew. She struggled with his sweater to reach more of him, to have all of him accessible to her.

With a growl of frustration Noble jerked the sweater up over his head, his fingers fumbling with hers as he tried to help her unbutton his shirt. They both released sighs of satisfaction when she could at last run her fingers through the thick, coarse hair on his chest.

A kiss, sweet and tender, was hers as Noble took hold of her forearms and pulled her to her knees. He held her close against his body, pressing her to his unyielding desire. A flush spread over her when his hands moved up the sides of her body, carrying her sweater and camisole along with them.

He tossed her clothing to one side and looked

down at her with dark, devouring eyes. He laid an almost reverent hand below one passion-engorged breast and caressed the hard tip with the pad of his thumb. Her senses reeled, and she closed her eyes. She felt drugged with pure bliss. His mouth took what his hand had discovered, sucking and tasting until she thought she might faint.

His hands were under her skirt. She could feel their heat through her panty hose as they roamed and explored, always keeping her close, holding her near.

"Damn, I hate these things," he muttered as his fingers tangled in the waistband of her stockings.

Wordlessly she opened her eyes, reached up under her skirt, and pushed her hose to her knees. She stood, never breaking contact with the fathomless dark eyes that held her enslaved to her own desires. She stepped out of her shoes and panty hose, then reached around to release the catch on her skirt, allowing it to fall away and pool at her feet. In panties alone she stood before him. Naked, vulnerable, and his for the taking.

Noble appeared awestruck as he stared at her. Reaching out blindly to untie his shoes, he then stood up to face her. He toed off his shoes while he unfastened his belt and released the zipper on his jeans. Quickly he removed his clothing to stand as bare and defenseless as she was.

"The first time I saw you, I knew you were someone very special, Emily. And I know it sounds strange, but I feel as if I've been waiting all my life for this moment," he said, his voice an intimate caress.

"Me too," she uttered. There was more to say, more she wanted to tell him, but the circuits in her mind were crossed and overloaded, leaving her speech center almost totally dysfunctional.

Words didn't seem important at the moment anyway.

In perfect parity they came together, their bodies yielding, their greedy hands laying claim to all they touched. Emily felt out of control. Nothing mattered to her except Noble's lips on hers, his mouth at her breasts, his hands as they moved low across her abdomen. A feathery caress along the inside of her thigh made her knees buckle and Noble eased her down to the blanket.

He sat up and removed her panties, his gaze taking in the full length of her nakedness. What had been a storm of passion in his eyes was now a raging tempest of urgent need. His kisses were hot and consuming. She arched and writhed against the exquisite torture he induced.

"Noble. Please," she cried out in desperation.

"Shh," he whispered as his hand scorched a path up her thigh to feed the fire within her.

Tidal waves of ecstasy washed through her, until at last she was washed away into a sea of oblivion. She floated there, content.

She felt Noble's hand gently stroke a line from her chin to the apex of her legs. Lazily she opened her eyes and forced heavy arms to reach out to him. His smile was gentle, adoring, and triumphant at once as he rose above her and entered the wet warmth she had prepared for him. With slow, easy thrusts he reignited the flames of excitement that had just begun to subside. Her need matched his in rhythm and pace, and together they found the ultimate peace.

"Emily?"

"Mmm?"

"Are you okay?"

"Mmm." It was the "mmm" of a deliciously limp and very contented woman. Noble had wrapped their damp, exhausted bodies in the other half of the blanket. As he held her gently with one arm around her waist, he fingered the stray curls at her temple with his other hand. Through some undefinable means he was conveying to her that he cherished her, and she felt it from the tip of her nose to the deepest depths of her soul. "I didn't know it could be like this."

"That's why our secret's so special. It can't be like this unless we share it. You and me. It wouldn't be the same with someone else."

"No, it wouldn't," she agreed sleepily. Noble made her feel important. He made her feel beautiful and more like a woman than she'd ever felt before. He listened to her opinions, respected her values, approved of her ambitions. When he spoke her name, it didn't sound like poor Emily or good ol' Emily. It came out *Emily*. Somebody very special. Somebody not ordinary or regular at all.

Seven

Emily's hand moved in a stealthy manner under the warm woolen blanket. Her fingers touched flesh and she pinched it as hard as she could. Slowly she opened her eyes. Noble was still there. He wasn't a dream or a fantasy. He was as real as the stinging pain in her arm.

She couldn't remember falling asleep, and she couldn't recall whether she'd had any dreams. But she was sure she'd never forget waking up and seeing Noble bent over the desk across the room. He was circled in lamplight, chewing on a pencil, frowning in confusion, and truly the most magnificent man she'd ever seen.

Where had this man come from, she marveled, acutely aware of the aching muscles in her love-strained body and the deep-seated serenity in her heart. How had he come by the power to change her life so completely in such a short time? Why did the life she'd been so satisfied with a week before seem so much more worth living now that he was in it? When had the lusty fascination with his body been overshadowed by something bigger and more significant? What would happen next?

She lay for a long time, warm and cozy in the blanket that still smelled of their loving, thinking and wondering. Her mind was a hodgepodge of pictures and questions. She had visions of a baby and a wedding, breakfasts for two, a big ugly dog with sad eyes, walks on a beach, breakfasts for four, cuddling and whispering in the dark, and Noble with gray hair.

She did some reconsidering about her trap too. How could she possibly go through with it now? She felt guilty already, and she hadn't even sprung it yet. Just the thought of her willingness to deceive him filled her with shame. She knew better than to listen to Jennifer. She knew better than to not listen to her own heart. A lie was a lie.

But what if Noble simply read William Joseph's papers and left? What if she were wrong? What if he wasn't feeling the same things she was? What if she couldn't hold his interest for longer than an afternoon? What if she were mistaken about the special bond between them? What if . . .

"So. You're awake, huh?" Noble had swiveled his chair in her direction. He was watching her closely, and she sensed a worried anticipation in his manner. It wasn't until he gave her a tentative, questioning little smile that she realized that in essence, this was their morning after. He was gauging her reaction to their impulsive lovemaking, to the fact that he knew what she looked like naked, and to the intimacies they had shared.

Emily found it hard to be anything but honest with him. She grinned at him and hoped he could see how happy she was.

"Hi," she said, her voice still deep with sleep.

"Hi, yourself," he said, returning her smile, his eyes telling clearly of his own joy and relief. "And women say men just roll over and start snoring."

"Was I snoring?"

Noble laughed. "No. But you're still very distracting when you're asleep."

"I am? Why?" Oh, Lord. Had she been grinding her teeth? Talking? Or worse?

"You look like an angel when you sleep. Peaceful and innocent. I like watching you, which made it almost impossible to concentrate on this stuff." He motioned to the papers on the desk.

Thank heaven, she thought. "Well, I'm glad you think I'm easier to look at than a bunch of hog reports. I told you they were dull reading," she said with a half laugh, pulling the blanket tightly about her as she came to a sitting position.

He curled his index finger at her and said, "Come here," in a way that made Emily shiver with anticipation. She got to her feet and walked slowly toward him, lured by the look in his eyes.

When she was within touching distance, he reached out and guided her hips gently into his lap. "Dull reading has nothing to do with the way you distract me."

To prove his statement, he kissed her thoroughly and didn't stop until she'd freed her arms from the blanket and was clinging to him with a need that matched his own. He cradled her in his arms for a while, seemingly content just to have her near him.

Emily couldn't remember feeling as solid and sure of herself as she was at that moment. She could feel his acceptance of and appreciation for who she was as if it were a tangible thing. He didn't ask or expect anything of her, didn't press her, and didn't try to mold her into something she couldn't be. He was gentle and cherishing. She wanted to live in his arms until the end of time.

"So, what do you think? Did my great-great-grandfather's pigs eat the gold, or is it all some mysterious code?" she asked after a while, secure enough to let time move on.

Noble gave her a discouraged half laugh as he idly thumbed the stack of papers. "I was so . . . preoccupied, I couldn't get into this earlier. But now that I've had a chance to really read it, I think you were right. This doesn't seem to be anything more than well-kept farm records." He chuckled. "He had nice penmanship though. I've tried to read some original documents that didn't look much better than chicken scratches done in ink. At least these are legible." And then, as if it were an afterthought, he absently added, "Unusual for a poor farmer in those days."

"But not so unusual for a schoolteacher," she said. When Noble looked at her, not understanding, she went on. "I thought you knew these weren't really written by my great-great-grandfather. He couldn't read or write. My great-great-grandmother taught him his numbers and how to add single-digits, but they say he couldn't find much sense in learning how to read and write when he had her and his sons to do it for him."

"That explains all the social notes in the margins and comments about their children's accomplishments."

"Not really. As I understand it, she was a very good and dutiful wife. She never wrote down anything in these records that he didn't tell her to. I think he made the comments about his sons because he was proud of them. Especially of their education. The social notes, as you call them, are time references. He knew the seasons and some of the months but specific dates were beyond him."

"Why didn't he just ask his wife what day it was?"

Emily shrugged. "Too easy, I guess. They say he was . . . mulish." She cast a wary eye at Noble. "You're not mulish, are you?"

"Who? Me? Never," he said, grinning. "My folks call me pigheaded and stubborn. But they've never called me mulish."

"Because you won't join the family law firm?"

He nodded. "Legal aid is beneath me. McEntires shouldn't associate with the common folk, you know," he said facetiously.

Emily pressed her cheek against his temple to show her understanding. "I have the same problem with Jennifer. She can't understand why I work for peanuts at the center when I could have kept my job in D.C. and made a lot more money. She doesn't seem to understand that the rewards of doing a job you care about can outvalue the pay."

He turned his head and placed a quick kiss of approval on her lips. "I like the way you think, Emily Becket."

We think alike, she noted mentally. In fact, the similarities in their lives and personalities were pretty amazing, now that she thought of it. Except for the fact that his ancestor was a Union crook and hers was a Confederate spy and war hero, and that his family was wealthier than hers, they'd taken parallel paths to homogeneous destinations.

They'd both fought against family opinion for careers that paid more in satisfaction than in money. They'd chosen jobs dealing with people who needed them. They were both intelligent, quiet-natured, and stubborn when their mind was made up.

They both had an interest in their lineage, were proud of it, and defended its honor. Emily ad-

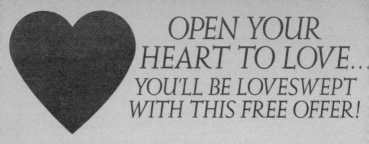

OPEN YOUR HEART TO LOVE...
YOU'LL BE LOVESWEPT WITH THIS FREE OFFER!

HERE'S WHAT YOU GET:

1. **FREE! SIX NEW LOVESWEPT NOVELS!** You get 6 beautiful stories filled with passion, romance, laughter, and tears... exciting romances to stir the excitement of falling in love... again and again.

2. **FREE! A BEAUTIFUL MAKEUP CASE WITH A MIRROR THAT LIGHTS UP!** What could be more useful than a makeup case with a mirror that lights up*? Once you open the tortoise-shell finish case, you have a choice of brushes... for your lips, your eyes, and your blushing cheeks.

*(batteries not included)

3. **SAVE! MONEY-SAVING HOME DELIVERY!** Join the Loveswept at-home reader service and we'll send you 6 new novels each month. You always get 15 days to preview them before you decide. Each book is yours for only $2.09 — a savings of 41¢ per book.

4. **BEAT THE CROWDS!** You'll always receive your Loveswept books before they are available in bookstores. You'll be the first to thrill to these exciting new stories.

BE LOVESWEPT TODAY — JUST COMPLETE, DETACH AND MAIL YOUR FREE-OFFER CARD.

mired Noble's efforts to clear his great-great-grandfather's name, even though he was trying to pawn the dirty deed off on her own relative. It was a hopeless but commendable cause that touched her heart.

It was his heavy, defeated sigh as he flipped the pages he'd read back on top of the pile that brought her thoughts back to the present. "I'm sorry you're not going to find what you came looking for," she said, her trap long gone from her mind. "I never could figure out why they kept all this stuff anyway. I mean, it's not likely that we'd need it for a tax audit after all these years." When her little joke failed to cheer him, she tried another approach. "At least you tried to clear his name, Noble. It was a long time ago. Don't you think it's best laid to rest and forgotten? It doesn't really have anything to do with you. Not personally, I mean."

"I know that. It's just always seemed like such a sad story of failure in a family full of overachievers. It would have been nice to right the wrong."

If it was a wrong, she added to herself, admiring his loyalty.

"I always hated the way it ended."

"How did it end?" she asked, not realizing she hadn't heard the end of the story.

"Well, it made him a little crazy trying to convince people that he was innocent. He eventually committed suicide."

"How awful. I'm sorry."

Noble laughed. "Lord, you're sweet. But as you said, it happened over a hundred years ago—too long to mean much to me." He turned earnest then, saying, "My life is in the here and now. And here and now I have . . . other things on my mind."

On his mind indeed, she thought as she giggled

in joyous expectation. She wiggled playfully in his lap and asked, "Such as?"

"I was hoping you'd give me a tour of the house."

"What?"

"A tour of the house. If you wouldn't mind, that is. It says here that it took him a week to build the main fireplace and chimney." He helped her to her feet and stood up beside her. "It's incredible to think that he actually stood here in this attic once. Do you ever get the feeling the place is haunted?"

"Ah, no," she said, trying to swallow her disappointment, feeling foolish for acting so wanton. "I've always had the feeling that all my people rest peacefully over in the churchyard." She paused. "This house does give me a feeling of being connected to something very old, though. Of being part of the line, like a link in a chain."

"And you're proud of that, aren't you?" he asked quietly, studying her face with interest.

She nodded. "Yes, I am. For the most part. But then, sometimes it feels like a great burden, you know?"

It was Noble's turn to nod his head, and she could tell by his facial features that he did understand. He knew how that warm, proud sense of belonging and being an intrinsic part of something could often take on great weight in responsibilities.

"How about that tour?" he reminded her softly.

"Yes, of course. If . . . if you'd like to go ahead, I'll get dressed and be down in a minute."

"You don't need your clothes, Emily," he said, walking over to the stairs that led to the lower floors.

Emily was stunned. Surely he didn't think she could lead him through the hallowed halls of the old ancestral home naked? A slow grin curled his lips, and white teeth sparkled as she stood there staring at him, aghast.

"In the first bedroom we come to, they'll just have to come off again," he said, wagging his brows lasciviously.

"Oh." Her spirits soared dramatically, and Noble laughed out loud. She could feel herself actually bouncing with eagerness as she walked across the room to join him. She hoped he wouldn't notice it too much. She sensed that being happy and willing were appropriate responses to what he was suggesting, and she was pretty sure that enthusiastic jumping and leaping was very uncool.

"Why do you keep it braided?" Noble asked as he ran his fingers through the mass of thick, coarse curls that fell about Emily's bare shoulders. "It's beautiful like this."

"I look like I've been struck by lightning—several times," she said, too tired to care what her hair looked like. But not so exhausted that she couldn't still enjoy the feel of his hands, the sound of his voice, and the fact that he liked how she looked.

The tour of the house had been short-lived, as Noble had insisted on seeing the second floor first. Two doors to the right of the attic stairs, he sauntered into the large corner bedroom that had belonged to Emily for as long as she could remember, and made himself at home. She followed him silently as he wandered about the cream and lavender colored room, looking at framed snapshots, reading book spines, and very obviously snooping in general.

"This must be your bedroom," he stated quite brilliantly, grinning at his own mental prowess.

"What was your first clue, Professor?"

"It looks like you," he said, closing the short distance between them. "Soft and feminine and very, very pretty."

He spread his hands wide against her cheeks, his fingers slipping into her hair. His gaze took in every aspect of her face possessively. Emily was a-twitter with the knowledge of what was about to happen. She could see the want and need in his eyes. She could feel him breathing faster and faster as his urgency spilled over and began to affect her as well.

"Ah, Emily," he uttered as if he were drowning in his own awe. "What's taken you so long?"

Emily didn't know what he meant by that, but then she didn't care as his mouth took hers in a complete and masterful way, draining all rational thought and emotions and replacing them with instinctive reactions and wild, untamed passions. She was only vaguely aware of him unbraiding her hair and removing the blanket, leaving her as free and natural as God had intended her to be.

Unfettered and with complete abandon she gave of herself to Noble. And when at last her body shut down, too exhausted to move, Noble was there to catch her. He held her limp, satiated body close to his and let the rhythm of his heartbeat pace hers along.

The sun that had long ago slipped away for the night was rising on the new day, but Emily paid it no notice. With her hands overlapped on his chest, she rested her chin between two knuckles and wallowed in the afterglow. Her body was warm and comfortable as it lay stretched out on top of him, her legs falling in the space between his.

"Then again," she added slowly. "I feel as if I've been hit by lightning. So I guess my hair finally suits the occasion."

Noble chuckled softly. "Your hair suits you all the time. Soft. Full of life. Wonderful."

Emily smiled. "You make me feel that way."

"Good. But I suspect you won't be feeling that way for long."

"Why not?"

"The sun's up, and you have to work today, don't you? You're not going to appreciate my keeping you up all night, once all this afterglow wears off."

"Oh, I don't know. I'm not exactly a brain surgeon, so I don't need to be in peak shape today. And I wouldn't have missed last night for anything," she said, resting her cheek on her hands, hoping he felt the same way.

He gave her a short, tight squeeze. "I'm glad you feel that way, because if it's up to me, this night will be only the first of many."

Emily sighed and resigned herself to his wishes. Oddly enough, her mind flashed back to those moments she had thought were the happiest of her life. They paled in comparison to this one. In fact, most of her memories seemed farther away than they had the day before. And the day before felt like a lifetime ago.

True, she was still the same ol' Emily with the job she loved and the house repairs to keep her busy. She was the same woman who could be counted on and trusted. And she still had a few basic insecurities. But something was different about her life. Everything was familiar but new. She'd come to a turning point during the night and crossed over to make a new start on her life.

"I'd better go," Noble said, breaking into her drowsy thoughts.

"What?"

"I said, I think I should leave." He didn't really sound as if he wanted to.

"Why? I want you to stay. It's nearly morning already, anyway."

"Emily, honey, you've got to get *some* sleep. So do I, for that matter. And frankly, I find it impossible with you in the bed."

"You do?"

"Ha," he said in disbelief, rolling her over and pinning her down with his body, a habit he had that she enjoyed very much. "Don't try to play innocent with me, you little witch. I can't keep my hands off you, and every time I touch you, I want you. And you know it."

Emily loved it. She looked into his eyes, and in her deepest, sexiest voice said, "You mean, like now?"

For an instant Noble looked startled. Then he grinned and groaned and buried his face in the hair at her neck. "Yes," he said with a growl against her throat, "like now."

Emily literally lived on love most of the day. She got drowsy by mid-afternoon but a slightly off-key rehearsal by her band of elderly musicians shook her out of that. With only one more day before their concert in the park, it was not the time to start getting sloppy.

"Well, who put a quarter in you," Bernie asked good-naturedly. "We weren't in tune Tuesday, and you said we were coming along just fine."

"I did?"

"Yes, ma'am. You said you were proud of us."

"I am proud of you. But that doesn't mean you don't have to try to stay in key with each other. You can do better than this. Now, come on. I want to show you all off on Saturday night. Okay, now—"

"To whom?" Bernie asked, breaking in as community spokesman.

"What?" Emily looked at all the avid faces. They

were watching her keenly, which led her to suspect that her feelings for Noble had been apparent all day.

"Who are you planning to show us off to?" Millie asked without the slightest bit of chagrin. "A new beau?"

"The whole town," she said emphatically.

"And a new beau?" Millie was a persistent sort.

When Emily didn't answer right away, Bernie asked, "You suppose that young McEntire fella who was here the other day finally caught up with her?"

Knowing smiles broke out on several faces, matching the one on Emily's.

"Oh, my," Gertie said with a sigh. "I had plans of my own for that one."

"Gert. Try picking on somebody your own age for a change," Bernie admonished her gently.

"Like you, for instance?" she asked Bernie, batting her eyes like a twenty-year-old coquette.

Bernie wagged his brows up and down at Gertie, much like Noble had at Emily the night before.

Emily giggled. "Okay. Let's get back to business here, people. Let's try 'Greensleeves' again. With everyone in the same key this time."

Bernie and Gert exchanged glances, then Bernie shrugged and said, "Some other time, Gertie, old girl. Right now I'm makin' music with Emily."

"Go back to sleep, you old fool," Gertie mumbled. "You've gotta be dreaming to think that I haven't heard that tired old tune before."

"All together now, please," Emily said again, sucking in her cheeks to keep from grinning. The cat-and-mouse game between Bernie and Gertie was an ongoing thing, and she'd never quite been able to figure out who was the cat and who was the mouse.

"Willard," Bernie said loudly at the man beside him, whacking his leg with his hand at the same time. "Turn your machine up so you can hear what you're playing. She wants us all in the same key this time."

Willard stared blankly at Bernie through thick horn-rimmed glasses for several seconds before he reached up and adjusted the hearing aid behind his left ear. Bernie nodded at him and then turned his attention back to Emily. "He doesn't hear any better out of his other ear. He needs two of those things."

Emily's nod was all the assurance he needed to know that a bug would be put in the proper person's ear to get the matter taken care of, and the rehearsal continued.

Emily heard the heavy steps on the stairs that led to her front porch. It wasn't hard to believe they were her own. She was almost numb with fatigue. Yet, incredibly enough, she was hoping to find Noble there waiting for her.

Neither one of them had been sure when they'd be free to see the other when they had reluctantly parted that morning. She'd been sure she wouldn't be home until after seven, and he couldn't remember if he had a study group scheduled for that evening or not. As tired as she was, she still had the energy to feel disappointment at not seeing him.

The folded note she found in her mailbox did much to lift her spirits and give her heart new hope.

Emily,
I do have a study group tonight.

Due to circumstances beyond my control,
I missed my morning run today.
I'll be running tonight. If your lights
are on, I'll stop. I've missed you all day.

Love,
Noble

Love, Noble? Emily hated letters that were signed
love, so-and-so. She was never sure what love
meant at the bottom of a letter. When Jennifer
signed that way, it meant one thing. When a close
friend did it, it meant something else. What did
Love, Noble mean? I like you, Noble? I don't know
how else to end this note, Noble? I'm nuts about
you, Noble?

A shower woke her up a little and gave her
enough stamina to wash the morning dishes. The
dishwasher was almost full when she remembered
the picnic basket and discarded clothing in the
attic and decided to go up and get them before
she forgot about them again.

Slowly she folded the blanket she and Noble had
made love on. Purposefully she let her mind daw-
dle on the memory of their lovemaking. Her heart
ached with a longing just to see him again.

She smiled wistfully and pondered the wonders
of the universe. It amazed her how things just
managed to happen sometimes. She'd known men
for months and years, and they'd never come close
to meaning as much to her as Noble had in less
than a week. It was almost as if they'd been meant
to be together, but the sun and the moon and all
the stars had to be in just the right positions in
order for them to meet. They were the right people in the right place at the right time.

"I love him," she uttered aloud, overwhelmed by
the sudden thought. It wasn't an infatuation with

his body anymore, and it didn't have anything to do with his handsome face—although they both factored into the overall feeling. But her feelings had gone beyond the physical. The churning excitement he stirred in her was far outweighed by the contentment in her heart at being accepted and valued for simply being herself. She felt a communion of their souls and a linking of their thoughts in the way they chose to live their lives.

"I really love him," she repeated, knowing in her heart that she always would.

As long as she was there, she decided to finish restoring the attic to its previous order. She carefully replaced her great-great-grandfather's papers in the airtight metal container that had kept them from deteriorating over the years. Again she had to wonder why anyone would keep all those meaningless records for so many years and finally settled on their sentimental value.

As far as she could see, it was the only reason she continued to care for them. They had little historical value and no monetary worth, but they'd been dictated by a Becket who had distinguished his name from all the others and started a family line to be proud of. They were part of her heritage, and for that reason alone she handled them gently.

That was when she noticed Noble's research papers on his own great-great-grandfather's plight. Wearily she flopped down into the wing chair and idly flipped through the pages. He'd spent a lot of time and energy digging up all the facts he had gathered, researching and validating each one before calling them true.

He'd brushed off his disappointment rather easily when nothing helpful in his quest to clear his relative had appeared in ol' William Joseph's papers. Was he really that objective about his project, or was he simply trying to be a good loser? If it were Emily who had gone so far only to come to a dead end, she would have been very disappointed, crushed even. Her heritage meant something to her. She was proud of it. And she couldn't shake the feeling that Noble felt the same way about his.

Without her glasses and without anything to munch on, she began to read.

In late April 1863, Lieutenant Noble McEntire was entrusted with a large shipment of gold and charged with the duty of procuring for the Union army sorely needed horses from the West. But before he could board the train which would start his journey to the Dakota territories, his command was attacked by a band of what appeared at the time to be other Union soldiers, and the gold was stolen. McEntire sustained a head wound that rendered him unconscious for most of the battle. He came to and discovered his small entourage dead to the last man. The chest that had contained the gold was empty, and six federal uniforms lay torn and discarded along the side of the road. He came to believe that the thieves had not been fellow Union soldiers after all, but southern Rebels dressed as such to ward off suspicion.

These Confederate raiders had been plaguing the countryside behind Yankee lines, inflicting great damage on the vulnerable flanks of the federal army. Their surprise attacks made short work of unsuspecting Union soldiers.

With a garbled story of the ambush and a fantastic story of Rebels in federal uniforms, McEntire returned to his company headquarters. Troops were sent out immediately to trail the marauding southerners. The posse returned to confirm the skirmish, the uniforms, and the trail of riders moving south, but they hadn't found the gold.

Eventually McEntire was suspected of setting the whole thing up and taking the money himself when no rumors or sign of the Confederates' use of the gold surfaced behind enemy lines. He was court-martialed, imprisoned, and later sent home in disgrace.

Emily studied the rough maps of the routes taken by the Union troops in pursuit of the stolen gold. They had trailed their quarry some forty miles from the point where McEntire was overtaken. Strangely enough, they'd tracked the raiders not three miles from where Becket House stood today, through a place called Lazy River Run.

"Emily?"

Noble's voice startled her. She hadn't realized how involved she'd become in the story. Reading the personal records of Noble's great-great-grandfather's trial and sentencing had moved her deeply, as the man professed his innocence throughout the entire procedure. There were tears in her eyes as she read his final entry, in which he still claimed to be blameless.

"Emily?" She could hear a note of concern in Noble's voice as he called up the stairwell into the attic. She opened her mouth to answer but had to clear the emotion from her throat before she could speak. "Emily? Are you here?"

"Yes. I'm here in the attic."

"Do you know that your front door is unlocked and that every light in the house is on?" he chastised her, his worry obvious, his tread rapid on the steps.

"Remount's not exactly crime infested, so I hardly ever lock the door. And I made a point of turning on all the lights so you'd be sure to see they were on."

He stopped at the top of the stairs and took a

casual stance with one hand on the railing. The grin on his face told her that her words had placated his fears and that her drain on the electric company's resources pleased him very much.

"Well, I saw. The place looks like a damn torch," he said with humor. He took in a deep breath and released it slowly. "Lord, I've missed you."

Emily wanted to scream and jump up and down. Would she ever get used to the way Noble looked? So handsome and strong. So cute and endearing. Her heart took flight at the thought that he actually cared enough about her to miss her. What *did* Love, Noble mean?

"I missed you too," she said quietly, knowing it sounded more like I love you from the tone of her voice. The two declarations were interchangeable. She wouldn't miss someone as much as she'd missed Noble if she didn't love them. Right?

With this said, and the undercurrent flowing hard and fast between them, there didn't seem to be much else to do but change the subject. Emily did her best.

"Aren't you afraid you'll catch cold, out running at night in just your shorts and that little T-shirt?"

It was like pouring lighter fluid on hot coals. The tension surrounding them doubled as she drew attention to his scantily clad body. She watched as his eyes took in her own bare feet and well-worn jeans. Her body quickened when his gaze came to rest halfway up her old, comfortable Remount T-shirt.

"I've been sort of hot all day. The cool air feels good," he said in an absent manner as his gaze came back to hers. His eyes still sparkled with feeling, but they weren't playful and glad anymore. They were intense and consuming. Suddenly he cleared his throat and stood up straight. "What are you doing up here?"

"Picking up," she said, motioning to the basket and small pile of clothes on the floor beside her, knowing they were both flashing back to the day before. "I got started reading this stuff and . . . well, you know, it's really very interesting. Did you know that Lazy River Run isn't more than three miles from here?"

He nodded as he walked over to join her, placing one thickly muscled and totally masculine calf on the armrest of her chair. "And the road the guerrilla fighters would have taken to Richmond would have led them to within half a mile of your front door. That's why, when I heard your great-great-grandfather's story, I thought it might be worth checking into. They could have made a quick detour here, left the money, and been back on track in just a few hours."

"You . . . ah . . . you've put a lot of time and thought into this investigation, haven't you, Noble?"

Again he nodded. "Maybe too much time. It started out as something interesting to do, but it's become more than that. A lot more than that. I feel as if I know the guy, and I want to prove his innocence so bad, I can almost taste it." He looked down at her and grinned. "Sounds stupid, doesn't it? The man's been dead for a hundred and twenty years, and whether or not he was guilty won't make a bit of difference to anyone but me, but . . . well, I don't know. I'd just like to know he was an honest man. I believe the words in his diary. I believe he was unjustly accused. I'd like to prove it."

"I understand," she said absently, thinking thoughts she knew she shouldn't have been thinking—such as how neatly her trap had been laid to make him think his great-great-grandfather was indeed innocent. And how it was still set up and waiting to be sprung. *And* how it wouldn't hurt anything or anybody to let him have his wild goose chase for the treasure, proving, one, that it had been stolen the way his great-great-grandfather said all along and, two, that it was long gone.

It wouldn't be the most honest thing she'd ever done, but it would certainly put Noble's mind to rest on the subject and ease his desire to prove that his namesake was an honorable man. Well, the decision to set the trap had been a hasty, self-indulgent one. The decision to spring it shouldn't be made the same way, she decided reasonably, even though her heart was leaning heavily toward this one piece of trickery to make Noble feel better.

"I know you understand," he was saying, "that's why I don't feel like a fool talking with you about it. Most people would laugh and say it was crazy to care."

"I don't think you're crazy."

"I'm not," he said, using his index finger to nudge a wayward curl back into place along her cheek. "Not about the past anyway. But I want you to know that I'm getting pretty crazy about you. I couldn't stop thinking about you all day."

"You couldn't?" she asked, fishing to hear more about this craziness, aware that he knew she was fishing.

"Nope." His smile was indulgent as he traced the shape of her lips with his index finger. "I kept thinking about how pretty you are, the way you taste, and how good it feels to hold you. I wondered what you were doing, if you'd fallen asleep on your feet yet . . . when I'd see you again."

"Me too," she said softly, wishing he'd scoop her up out of the chair and carry her off to the bedroom.

He kissed her gently, repeating the kiss over and over at her request, leaving her limp and longing for more.

Hardly breaking contact, he stood and gathered her up in his arms. He looked down once at the top of the stairs to get his bearings, then returned to pleasing Emily, even before the magic of his kisses had time to wear off.

They spent a second night in the throes of their passion, sharing secrets in the dark, trading memories and dreams. They even slept for a while, waking with the sunshine to partake of their love once again.

Eight

The next day Emily felt as if she were the rope in a tug-of-war. One minute the trap was out of the question because it was dishonest and deceitful. The next minute it was an act of love and kindness.

She made her final decision that night. Noble sat across from her in a quiet little restaurant, telling her about his family and the way he was brought up.

"Even my brother, who chases windmills for a profession, thought I was nuts to come all the way down here to try and vindicate my great-great-grandfather," he said. "It was his idea that I teach a class while I was here, so it wouldn't be a total waste of my time."

"What do you mean, he chases windmills?"

"Well, the clients you get in the public defender's office aren't always the most innocent people in town. Even if they've confessed to him that they committed the crime, my brother gives them a gung-ho defense—and usually gets them off. He says that if you don't give the guilty the best defense possible, the truly innocent don't stand a chance at a fair trial. *Everybody* deserves to get the best defense."

"And you agree with him," she said, knowing it to be true because he'd told her so before.

He nodded as he chewed, and when he could speak, he said, "But I'm not nearly as patient and virtuous as Ted. It drove me nuts trying to defend repeat offenders and people who, in my heart, I knew ought to be locked up forever. So I chose legal aid work because the people there, for the most part, are solid citizens who would spend their last penny hiring big, expensive firms like my family's to prove their innocence. With us, they pay what they can and keep their homes and their pride intact."

Emily loved the way he understood pride. It was something she had more than her fair share of and something she dealt with every day. The people she worked with had pride too. Nothing hurt more than being overlooked because they were old. Nothing was more humiliating than to be condescended to because they were past their prime. Nothing was more degrading than to have their words ignored simply because their bodies could no longer keep up with their brains.

"Is it going to be hard for you to go back and face him with nothing to show for your time here?" she asked.

He shrugged. "He's made his share of mistakes. I'll have plenty of ammo to defend myself with when he starts razzing me." He smiled. "Besides, once he sees what I've discovered here, he'll shut his mouth fast enough."

"What you've discovered?"

"You." He said the word as if he'd meant to say rubies and diamonds, and Emily felt a tingling heat rush into her cheeks.

She wasn't rubies and diamonds. She was simply Emily. But if he wanted to think so, she wasn't about to set him straight. And for all the happiness he'd brought into her life, thinking the way he did and acting on his thoughts, he deserved some happiness in return. She couldn't let him face his brother and have his pride wounded with nothing to show for his endeavors.

The trap would give him all the proof he needed to show that his instincts about his great-great-grandfather had been correct.

"So you'll come? And you won't laugh if they're a little out of tune?" Emily asked Noble later as she brought the popcorn into the front parlor and glanced at the television to see which movie they'd be watching.

"I wouldn't laugh."

Emily knew that. She was just trying to prepare him, let him know that it might not be the best concert he'd ever heard. Actually she was eager to see how he and her friends from the center would get along. This was the first time anyone who really meant anything to her had shown an interest in what she did for a living. It would be the first time her friends would meet someone who was important to her. She wanted to show off one to the other. She was proud of all of them, and she wanted it to go well.

Emily sighed and gave Noble a long, considering look while he got comfortable on the couch. There was no sense in putting it off. If she was going to do it, if she was going to spring the trap, there was no better time than the present.

"Would you like a fire?" she asked.

He grinned up at her, and there was no mistaking his thoughts as he nodded. "Want me to make it?"

"No. It's all set. All I have to do is light it."

"Always prepared, with picnics and fires. You must've been one hell of a little girl scout."

"Boy scouts are always prepared. And I was a Sunshine girl."

"I believe that," he said, watching her put the long, narrow match to the paper and kindling under the grate that contained three large pieces of wood.

She fiddled with the fire for as long as she could before finally standing to put the match box back on the mantel, which like the rest of the fireplace was made of the same stone as the exterior of the house.

Her great-great-grandfather had taken weeks to painstakingly lay each rock in the huge fireplace exactly where he wanted it. As a result, it stood solid and firm, weathering the years of use and service it was intended for.

"Oh. Will you look at that." Emily tried to make her voice sound surprised and disheartened at the same time. "There's a crack in the mortar here around this stone. I swear this place is going to fall down around my ears before I ever get the stairwell repapered. Oh, this is awful. I wonder how much it'll cost to repair it."

She'd shown just enough alarm and despair to get Noble back on his feet and over to the fireplace to examine it. The rest of the trap she left in the hands of fate.

"It doesn't seem so bad," he said, taking a close look at the mortar around the rock. "It'll hold. This thing is so old, I'm surprised this is the only . . . oh, jeez. What's this? It's loose."

Emily tried to match the astonishment in her

expression to that in Noble's when he pulled the rock out of the fireplace. "Noble. Don't tear the whole fireplace apart."

"I didn't. I'm not," he said disjointedly. "I only jiggled it a little, and the damn thing just came out." He peered into the hole left by the stone just as she had expected him to. "There's a hole here."

"Well, of course, Noble. You take a rock out of a stone fireplace, and it's bound to leave a hole. You're not exactly real good with your hands, are you?"

He stopped in mid-motion and gave her an inane stare. "That's not what you said this morning, honey. Come here. Look. The space is bigger than the hole left by the rock."

Emily let him show her the deep, dark hole that went well inside the fireplace. She screwed her face into a puzzled frown. "Well, what is it? Part of the flue?"

"No. It can't be. It's in the wrong place. It looks as if it were made on purpose; the edges are all smoothed over. It looks like a secret hiding place or a hidden vault."

"It can't be," she said. "We already have one of those." He looked at her then, expecting her to go on. "Well, it's not really a vault or anything. And it's no secret anymore, because it's plainly visible in the old sketches of this place. Everyone who's ever been to the attic to go over William Joseph's papers has come down to tell us about the hidden room under the stairs. And, of course, we've always known about it. William Joseph had it built into the house as a place to put the women folk in case we were ever invaded again by the North. It hasn't been used in years."

"Are you kidding me?" he asked, straight-faced.

"No. I saw it once when I was young. There's a

bunch of boxes in there now, but my mother told me what it was for."

Noble laughed, and she laughed with him. "Well, your old William Joseph didn't miss a trick, did he?" he said, turning back to his discovery. "A hidden room to protect the women from rape, and a secret vault to protect himself against pillage and plundering. A real trusting fellow, that one. And how long after the war was this house built?"

"Oh, about ten or fifteen years or so."

"And all that time he was waiting to be 'reinvaded' from the North?" He laughed again, shaking his head, apparently trying to make up his mind whether he wanted to stick his hand into the dark recesses of the hole to investigate. "Do you suppose there's anything in there? Or was it left empty in readiness for the invasion?"

"Beats me." It was her turn to look into the hole dubiously. Should she have left part of the paper showing, she wondered?

"Do you want me to check and see?"

"Well, I'm not going to stick my hand in there. I don't like bugs I can't see."

Slowly Noble reached his hand inside, and with an expression of sheer awe, he pulled out a folded slip of paper.

"Look," he said, his eyes lighting with wonder. "This has been in there all this time, and no one even knew about it."

"Except whoever put it there," she pointed out.

"Obviously your great-great-grandfather, since he was the one who built the fireplace and put in the hidden vault."

He carefully opened the thin, yellowed piece of paper, then frowned. "It's just more of that stuff from upstairs. . . . No. Wait. This was written in the spring of 1863. The papers upstairs didn't start until a year later."

"Well, what does it say?"

"The usual stuff. There are a lot of 'Yanks took' here. It must have been a bad year, with the federal troops taking so much of his food and livestock to feed themselves."

"But that sort of thing went on until 1865. What's so unusual about this particular time period that he'd put it in the fireplace and lock it away?" she asked, encouraging him to examine the document more closely.

Noble shook his head. "The only social note is 'six of Lee's boys came to use the well last night.' "

"Lee's boys? Confederate soldiers?"

"Sounds like it. They must have stopped for water."

"So?"

"Well, maybe this trusting soul of an ancestor of yours didn't want any evidence left behind that he'd aided Rebel troops. Maybe he hid this paper in here so it wouldn't be found when the place was reinvaded. It's the only reason I can think of for hiding this one particular report where no one would ever find it."

That wasn't the conclusion she'd wanted him to come to, but any further prodding on her part might arouse his suspicion. "Mmm. Maybe," she said, giving her dilemma more consideration. This definitely threw a wrench into the smooth operation of her plan, but it wasn't hopeless yet.

Before she had time to come up with an alternate plan to get Noble to make the conclusions she wanted him to, fate stepped in and took over.

Noble sent a searching hand back into the dark hole, obviously checking to make sure the vault was completely clean of its secrets. "I can't believe he'd go to the trouble of making this hidden space for one lousy piece of paper. He can't have been . . . Emily."

"What?"

"There's something here. Another hole, no, it's a false bottom."

"A what?"

"This vault has a false bottom in it. Look, it lifts right out," he said, withdrawing a thin piece of slate from the hole in the fireplace and showing it to her.

Emily hardly noticed the excitement in his face. Her family had known about the vault in the fireplace for decades. It had been the only family secret they'd been able to conceal under repeated close scrutiny, as it hadn't been drawn into the original plans for the house as the secret room had been, and it was virtually undetectable to the uninformed observer. Noble's discovery was a huge shock to Emily.

"Are you sure?"

"Of course I'm sure. Look. Shall we see what's in it?"

A feeling of impending doom swept over Emily. Suddenly she felt as if she'd stepped into a mystery movie or a sci-fi thriller. If Noble disturbed the contents of the concealed chamber, she was sure they'd be cursed until the end of time or killed instantly by some horribly gruesome alien that had been locked in there for the last century.

"No."

Noble looked at her. He frowned at her strange behavior and asked, "Why not?"

"Because." She began to wring her hands nervously.

"Emily. Why not?"

"Because we don't know what's in there. It could be anything."

"We didn't know what was in the hole before, did we? And it turned out to be a useless piece of paper. Who's to say this won't be more of the same?"

Who's to say, indeed, she repeated mentally. She easily sidestepped the fact that one of them *had* known what was in the primary cavity. How could she tell him she had planted it there for him to find? But she couldn't get around the sick feeling in the pit of her stomach that told her they were meddling with the past. They'd blundered across something that was never meant to be found. They'd disturbed a dead person's secret . . . there had to be something mystically dangerous about that. The whole thing was beginning to give her the creeps.

"It won't be, Noble. If there's anything down there, it won't be good. Why else would someone go to the trouble of putting it in a hidden chamber inside a hidden chamber? Let's just put the rock back and forget the whole thing."

"Emily," he said, clearly confused by her behavior. "Aren't you the least bit curious as to what's in there?"

"No." She shook her head for added confirmation.

"Well, I am. I'll go nuts if you don't let me see what it is. Tell you what, we'll flip a coin. Heads we look, tails we forget it."

Emily didn't want to flip a coin. She didn't want to know what was in the hole. But she didn't have anything to argue her point with except the unreasonable fear that all her teeth would fall out if they disturbed the contents of the secret hiding place.

Noble flipped the coin and it landed with George Washington's face up. An army of willies marched down Emily's spine.

"Emily honey, don't look so scared," Noble said, smiling at her foolishness, his arm almost elbow deep into the hole. "I promise if it's something horrible, like a confession of guilt from ol' William Joseph, we'll burn it and leave the legend intact," he added, teasing her with his theory that her great-great-grandfather had received the stolen shipment of gold.

Her great-great-grandfather's innocence or guilt was the furthest thing from her mind at the moment. She was waiting for the walls of the house to start crumbling down around them or for Noble to let out a death cry and pull back a bloody stump of an arm from the hole. She almost fainted with relief when he brought out several sheets of folded paper, and the house didn't even quiver in response.

"What is it?" she uttered, holding her breath, watching as Noble blew the dust from his find.

The papers were obviously old and frail, not having the benefit of airtight containers to preserve them. They were darkly yellowed with age and very dry, and the edges began to fall off in Noble's gentle fingers.

"What is it," she asked again, her curiosity and enthusiasm growing naturally.

"I can't tell. It looks like a letter, but the ink is so faded, I can hardly read it."

Noble laid the pages out on a small side table while Emily turned on the lamp at the other end.

The bleached ink came to life under the light, and handwriting familiar to Emily was legible.

" 'To whom it may concern,' " he read. With a beaming grin he glanced at Emily and said, "That's us."

"Just read it," she said, impatient.

Noble cleared his throat and studied the page silently for several seconds before he began to read aloud.

" 'My name is Maggie Becket. I am the first and, hopefully, only wife of William Joseph Becket. I write at this time to tell of an event that I feel needs to be told. My husband is a good but stubborn man and refuses to make a proper record of it. To protect his honor and his name, I feel it necessary to disobey his wishes. I can only hope that this does not fall into the wrong hands and put him in danger.

" 'On the eighteenth day of April in the year 1863 six men came to our homeplace in the dark of night. With my husband's wounds from the war not yet completely healed, I grew worried when he went out to face them alone. I sent our oldest son out to watch over his father and to try to protect him, if necessary. My son returned to say that the men were Confederate soldiers and were familiar to my husband. He said there were two at the dry well near the west field and four in the barnyard, talking in friendly tones with his father.' "

Noble paused thoughtfully and looked down at Emily with a shine of triumph in his eyes. "My great-great-grandfather's entourage was attacked on April sixteenth. Emily, this could be it."

Emily was too caught up in the moment to know how to answer. She was fascinated by the letter from a woman, long dead, who prior to this time had played only a small part in the background of the Becket family history. Noble continued to read when she made no response.

" 'My husband was angry that I had sent the boy out to help him, but after much discussion on my part, he finally told me why the soldiers had come and then swore me to secrecy.

" 'As I have promised my husband, I will never speak of that night, but I firmly believe that the truth should be told someday. My husband would take it to his grave, but I feel no such loyalty to anyone but him, and it is for his sake that I set down the facts now.

" 'A Lieutenant Gerald Wakeland and five of his men—Pitney, Finney, Hansen, and two others whose names I can't recall—brought a stolen shipment of Union gold to my husband, and he allowed them to put it in the dry well near the west field for safekeeping. They are to return soon and take it away, but I cannot feel easy about it. Union troops abound in this area at present. If the secret in the well were to be discovered, the consequences would be grave, especially for my William Joseph.' "

"There. I knew it," Noble exclaimed in exaltation. He picked Emily up and twirled her around the room until she was dizzy, saying, "He was innocent. He told the truth all along. He was innocent."

"Noble. Noble. You didn't finish. You didn't finish the letter. What else does it say? Put me down and let me read it," she said, laughing, trying to catch her breath.

"Oh, who cares? She told us everything we needed to know. This is like solving the ultimate crime. No evidence, no witnesses, nothing. And still justice prevails and the truth comes out." Noble was being dramatic in his high emotional state at finally uncovering the truth about his great-great-grandfather. He reminded Emily of a

little boy on Christmas morning, concerned only
with getting what he'd wished for.

When she was finally able to break away from
him, she went back to the table and began to read
where he'd left off.

" 'It has been many months now since my
husband's friends came and left the gold at
the bottom of the well. William Joseph is beginning to fear that something has happened
to them and that they might not ever return.
He gave his word that the money would never
fall into Yankee hands again and that it would
be used for the good of the South.

" 'He has made several attempts to contact
other loyal Confederates who might be of some
help in getting the gold to the proper authorities, but the conditions of the war make travel
and communications difficult.

" 'No matter the outcome, my husband will
remain faithful, but I grow more resentful
with each passing day. I cannot forgive those
who left my husband with this burden and in
such great danger. It was Lieutenant Wakeland
who instilled the value of a child's education
in my husband, when even I had failed to do
so. But even for this I cannot thank him, in
light of what he has done.' "

The room grew ominously silent as the final
words hung in the air on a bitter note. Emily and
Noble looked at each other. Their gazes met and
held meaningfully.

"They didn't come back for it," Emily whispered
into the silence.

Noble remained quiet a while longer, then asked,
"Do you think it's still out there somewhere?"

Emily was afraid to nod her head; it just bobbed on its own accord. She didn't want to believe that thousands of dollars in gold had been under her nose—or, more accurately, under her feet—since the day she was born, that the rumor was true and she was the clever Becket to uncover it . . . with the help of a McEntire, of course. She fought the urge to slap herself alert, knowing it would be a useless gesture, not to mention painful.

"Are there any dry wells left on your property that you know of?" Noble asked, his voice soft as if he, too, were trying not to dispel the magic thoughts passing back and forth between them.

The dry well under the gazebo in the backyard popped into her mind like a stripper out of a cake at a bachelor party. She tried to caution herself with the possibility that other dry wells existed, but it was no use. It was too much of a coincidence, she told herself. It was the same well she'd been going to lead Noble to in the trap she'd set for him. Nah. It couldn't be the same well, she decided. That would be too easy.

"There . . . there are some old maps and drawings upstairs—" she said, stopping mid-sentence as Noble jumped up, grabbed her hand, and had her halfway to the second floor before she could take another breath.

Nine

Emily stifled a yawn with the back of her hand.
Her eyes burned, and her neck was stiff from
poring over the old sketches of what once had
been the Becket farm, then the Becket estate, and
more recently Becket House, Remount College, and
its grounds.

She had long since given up the fight with her
intuition. She knew the well they were looking for
was under the gazebo, but instead of telling Noble
outright that she knew where it was, she remained
silent. Taking the time Noble used in his extensive and zealous search for the well, she tried to
reconcile herself to the revelations in her great-
great-grandmother's letter.

Temporarily setting aside the creepy feelings she
had about encountering the words of a woman
who'd been dead for nearly a century, trespassing
on her privacy, and revealing her secrets, there
was still the matter of the treasure to get used to.
It really existed.

Before, it had been an amusing delusion to think
about on a hot, sunny afternoon when nothing

truly seemed real to begin with. It had been entertaining to daydream about finding it, but Emily had never put any solid faith in its existence. But now . . . now she had to. It wasn't a rumor or a fairy tale any longer. It was real. And everything she'd thought to be the truth had to be revised in her heart as well as in her mind.

It had happened just as Noble had suspected. Her great-great-grandfather had been part of the conspiracy to rob from the North and give to the South. Well, that wasn't so bad, she decided. It was wartime, after all, and faithful Confederates did what they could for the cause. She might have done the same in his place.

The wrongful conviction of Noble's great-great-grandfather and his subsequent death was a hard lump to swallow, though. His crisis was suddenly more real to her than before. Noble had said that he'd "gone a little crazy, trying to prove his innocence" and she could well imagine how that had happened. Could there be anything more frustrating or discouraging than knowing the truth and not being able to prove it? Could there be anything more humiliating or degrading to an honorable man than to be unjustly accused of a crime he didn't commit? Emily didn't think so, and her heart ached for him.

Still, she couldn't put her own ancestor in a dim light. How could he have possibly known about the first Noble McEntire's plight? And even if he had, could a soldier be expected to stand up for his enemy? Shamefully, she had a feeling it would rarely happen. Her great-great-grandfather wasn't anything more than a mortal man. A farmer-soldier-family man, not a superman. If he'd confessed to having the gold during the war, he'd have been a conspirator to one side and a traitor to the other. If he'd talked about it after the war, he still would have risked great danger to his entire family. Leaving the stolen gold deep in the well for the future to deal with had been a wise and prudent decision on his part. And Noble's great-great-grandfather? Well, whoever said that all was fair in love and war was obviously right. Emily felt sorry for him but had to believe that it had all turned out the way fate had ordained it.

Noble removed his glasses and tossed them gently onto the desk in front of him. He looked worn out. His eyes had lost the shine of excitement they'd had earlier and were beginning to show the strain he'd put on them trying to pinpoint the magic well with the pot of gold at the bottom of it from the faded old pictures and sketches spread out before him.

He rubbed his eyes with his thumb and index finger, then looked over at Emily. His expression softened dramatically before he spoke. "Sleepy?"

She nodded.

"Well, I think we've got it narrowed down to two possibilities here," he said, leaning back in the chair. "According to these drawings, there were only two wells on the original property at the time this all happened. And my best guess is that this house stands in the middle of what was actually their west field. Sooo . . . the well in question shouldn't be too far from here."

"It's under the gazebo in the backyard," she stated flatly.

He gave her a peculiar look and dumbfoundedly asked, "How do you know that?"

"I saw the opening once when I was younger, but I didn't really know what it was. I've lived here all my life, and it's the only hole in the ground I know about."

"Well, why didn't you tell me this sooner?"

"I don't know," she said, getting to her feet. "Don't you have sort of an unreal feeling about this? I'm finding it very hard to believe."

"No. Not really. But then, I didn't grow up thinking of it as a rumor." He paused. "It seems plausible to me because it's what I thought all along. But that still doesn't explain why you didn't tell me about the well. Don't you want to find the gold?"

She shrugged. "It's not that. I had this sick feeling in my stomach that everything I've believed to be true all my life was suddenly not the truth at all. I needed time to think, and I wanted the chance to eliminate any other possibilities. I can't believe I came so close to it and didn't even know it." She gave a small, thoughtful laugh as something else occurred to her. "You know what? I can't count the times I've heard someone in my family complain about the positioning of the gazebo. There would have been more shade and a better view if they'd built it on the other side of the house."

"When was it built?"

Emily gave him a conspirator's smile. "After William Joseph died, Maggie had it built. They say she used to sit there for hours, soaking up the morning sunshine."

Noble wagged his brows knowingly. "Guarding the treasure would be more like it."

"Or plotting revenge against the men who left it and caused my great-great-grandfather so much turmoil and worry."

"She must have been a pretty gutsy lady to have disobeyed her husband like that, to write the testimonial to his involvement to protect him in case it was ever found out. Are all you Becket women so loyal to your men?"

"If we love them, yes."

Silence crackled between them like a live wire, and the air grew thick with tension as Noble sat staring at her. There was a warmth in his eyes that had become very familiar to Emily. A look she knew she would miss in the deepest parts of her soul, if it were ever to disappear. A look so special and unique, it made her feel treasured and cherished above all else. A look she didn't want to live without, ever again.

She didn't move when he rose from the chair and walked toward her. She trusted completely the hands that reached out for her. She moved freely into his embrace. She gave herself up to the lips that pressed hot, soft, and urgently against hers. And with all her might, she tried not to look disappointed when the kiss slowly ended.

With his index finger under her chin, he lifted her face to his once more. "Emily, if you don't feel right about going after the gold, we don't have to."

"What? And leave it in the well for another century?" she asked, confused. "Why?"

"Well, you said this whole thing was making you feel strange. I just wanted you to know that you have an option. We can forget about it, or, at the very least, we can take a few days to get used to the idea of it being real before we dig it up. It's not going to go anywhere." He looked into her eyes with concern and understanding. "I don't want you to feel obligated to dig it up just because I know about it. If you want to let the legend remain as it is, I'll keep your secret. The letter is enough for me. I have all the proof I came for, and it doesn't have to go any further than the two of us."

"You mean you'd be willing to give up all that gold?"

"Well, it's not as though we're going to get any of it anyway. We'd end up donating it to some national museum or something, and all we'd get for our trouble is our names in the paper . . . and maybe a small finder's fee. But we're not going to end up filthy rich by digging it up. And it's certainly not worth turning your whole world upside down for."

Emily thought about his proposal and was deeply touched.

"It's not going to make that much difference in my life, I guess. Everyone knows William Joseph . . . did things during the war that he could have been hanged for. This will prove it and bring an end to the rumors and folklore about the treasure of Becket House. At least that will put an end to all the stupid professors marching up here to read those damned farm records."

"Stupid professors?" His brows rose in mock indignation.

Emily gave him a teasing grin and quickly slipped out of his reach, heading for the stairwell. "In and out. In and out. They're such a bother. Up here till all hours, trying to decode the weight of a hog's body." She paused. "Actually, I'll probably miss them. There have been a couple of very cute scholars over the years. There was one in particular that I liked very much. . . ."

"There was?" Noble asked, breaking in on her rambling, showing a decided interest.

"Mmm. I could hardly keep my hands off him."

"Oh, yeah? And where was he from?"

Noble looked so confident in her answer that Emily couldn't resist saying, "Minnesota."

"Minnesota?" he asked, his expression lowering into a sharp frown.

"Or was it Philadelphia?" she wondered aloud,

grinning. "There've been so many, it's hard to recall."

"Yeah? Well, maybe he just didn't leave a deep enough impression?" he said, stealthily making his way toward her. "Maybe he should have taken his time and made sure that you'd never, ever forget who he was or where he came from."

"Mmm. Maybe," she said, moving down onto the steps, ready to flee. "But you know how hard it is for those smart types to make themselves stand out in a crowd. They're so socially awkward, only their mothers could really love them."

"That does it," he said with a growl, rushing her and missing her at the top of the stairs. "I'm going to socially-awkward you when I catch you, Emily. I'll show you how we smart types make ourselves stand out."

"You're going to read to me?" she called over her shoulder, giggling, not daring to stop as she taunted him.

"Not exactly," he said, lunging for her at the bottom of the stairs. Missing her by a fraction of an inch, he took a header to the floor, landing heavily on his hands and knees.

Emily momentarily halted, her concern for Noble her downfall. He was already on his feet and looming up beside her before she could make another getaway. He grabbed her at the waist with both hands and turned her around to face him.

"You'd better stop that giggling and sober up, woman. You're about to learn the lesson of your lifetime."

"Whoa. This oughta be good."

Noble nodded slowly and smiled licentiously.

"It'll be good," he said, backing her into her bedroom. He closed the door with one backward kick of his foot, and Emily dissolved in giggles of delight.

• • •

Emily hated waking up to the harsh clanging of an alarm clock. She much preferred the soft Saturday voice in her head that nagged at her gently and whispered that she'd slept long enough.

She stretched her body from head to toe slowly, arousing her senses to the new day. Her hand slid across the cool linen that hadn't been warmed with body heat, seeking the warmth that had comforted her throughout the night.

"Noble?" she called, her voice still groggy with sleep as she realized she was alone in the bed.

"I'm here," he said. The bed sagged heavily to one side, and he was beside her again, even before her eyes had adjusted to the light of the early morning sun. He gave her a quick smack on the mouth and asked, "What's my name and where am I from?"

"Noble James McEntire," she spouted readily, grinning and recalling the in-depth education she'd received during the night. "Philadelphia."

"Good girl. You ever going to forget that?"

"Never, ever," she said, putting her arms around his neck, confirming her words with a promissory kiss.

"Lord, you're pretty," he muttered more to himself than to her as he absently twisted one of her unruly brown curls around his finger. "I don't ever want to roll over in bed and not find you there. I'm falling in love with you, Emily. I like having you in my life."

In a dreamlike state, where gestures symbolized emotions, Emily tenderly palmed his cheek with her hand. He leaned into it, watching her closely, unable to hear her vows to love and cherish him always as they sprang from her heart.

"Huh. You're speechless," he said with the short

little half laugh of someone unaccustomed to declaring his finest feelings and getting no response. "I'm moving too fast again, aren't I?"

"No. You're moving just right. I feel as if I've known you forever. It's already hard for me to remember what life was like without you."

"And I can't imagine mine any other way."

Their kiss was a clarification of what they'd both known the minute they'd set eyes on each other. They belonged together. Their life forces had been destined to join since the beginning of time. They'd never have to fight the world alone again. They'd never be lonely or solitary again. In each other they'd found their soul mate, their heart's desire, their mental companion. They found the right to their left, the night to their day, the top to their bottom. It was a very long, satisfying kiss.

Noble flopped back on the bed, winded and obviously fighting for control, although Emily wasn't sure why. Controlling his desire for her wasn't something he did well, and that suited her just fine.

"Okay," he said, breathless. "We have a choice here. We can stay in bed and make wild, wonderful love to each other all day—which has my personal vote of approval. Or we can get up and check out that well."

"Hmm. That is quite a choice."

"*Or*," he said, coming up on one elbow enthusiastically. "You can let me make love to you in the shower, and *then* we can go treasure hunting."

"Ha. Leave it to a lawyer . . ."

"We might have to tear the gazebo down," Noble was saying as he crawled back out from under the old dilapidated structure. "The opening has shrunk, and there's probably dirt down inside too. I won't be able to dig if the gazebo doesn't come down first."

"Well, at least it'll save me the expense of having it repaired and painted this summer," she said, trying to inject at least a small amount of hidden regret into her voice. At the same time, she was trying not to feel too guilty in knowing that she'd intended for the gazebo to come down long ago. It had been neglected of late and was in a very sad state of disrepair. Her original plan had been to have Noble help her tear it down during his wild goose chase anyway. Thank goodness for Maggie's letter, she thought, sending a prayer heavenward. At least she didn't have to feel guilty about lying to Noble any longer. The trap could remain her secret, and she didn't need to feel bad about it.

The two of them spent the rest of the morning and most of the afternoon taking the roof and sides off the gazebo. Noble had tied one end of a rope to one of the support beams on the gazebo, and the other to the rear bumper of his car. It had taken very little effort to coax the rotten wood into a heap of rubble.

With a hammer and a lot of beautiful muscle flexing, which Emily enjoyed very much, Noble broke the structure up into small pieces for Emily to carry away. Twilight was setting in as her muscles began to protest their abuse. She had a few small slivers in her hands, but their discomfort was far outweighed by the ache in her arms and shoulders and the throbbing low in her back. She sat down wearily on the steps of the now-gone gazebo and didn't bother to stifle a groan of fatigue.

"Lord, woman, will you look at yourself," Noble scolded, an expression of exaggerated disgust and disbelief on his face. "I just finished bathing you, and you're a mess again already."

Emily looked down at her filthy jeans and sweatshirt, feeling the grit and grime on her skin and in her hair. She looked back at Noble, who was dirtier than she was, in what she thought to be a beautifully sweaty male way, and innocently said, "Gee, Dad, I don't know how this happened. I've just been sitting here all day."

Noble chuckled and jumped down off the platform, all that was left of the old gazebo. "Well, I think we've done a good day's work. I'm beat. I vote we quit for the day and go in and take another shower."

"Together?" she asked with childlike hopefulness.

"Of course."

"Oh. Wait a second," she said, suddenly alarmed. She picked up Noble's arm to look at the time on his watch. "The concert in the park. I almost forgot it."

"We have time. But I think I'd better go back to my apartment and change clothes again. If I'd remembered this morning, I could have brought my clothes with me when I changed into my grubbies."

"Sorry. I should have reminded you," she said, taking in the broad shirtless expanse of his chest and shoulders, wondering if she'd ever get over the giddy feeling she got when she looked at him.

"We were . . . preoccupied this morning," he said in that tone of voice he had that was so like an intimate caress. He helped her to her feet and draped his arm around her shoulders. Together they walked back toward the house with hardly a second thought for the fortune in gold that lay beneath the ground only a few feet away from them.

As if by silent mutual agreement they both realized there was no need to take any precautions in safeguarding the treasure. It would be there whenever they felt like digging it up. Since they were the only two people in the world who knew about it, and they trusted each other implicitly, what possible harm could come to it?

"Jennifer. I really can't talk right now," Emily told her cousin for the second time. "I'll call you tomorrow and tell you all about it."

"No, you won't. You're so ga-ga over this guy, you can hardly remember your own name, let alone mine. You'll forget to call, and I'll be stuck here by the phone all day waiting for it to ring." She paused and then took a new approach. "Look. You don't have to tell me everything. I didn't just crawl out from under a rock, you know. Just give me some of the high points, and I'll draw my own conclusions."

Emily laughed. Jennifer probably had her relationship with Noble all figured out by now, just from her reluctance to talk about it. What she really wanted was to hear all the finer details, and Emily didn't want to share those with anyone but Noble. Still, she knew she'd never be dressed and ready to go when Noble came for her if she didn't throw Jennifer a few scraps of meaty information to chew on. "What would you call a high point?"

"Well," she started, obviously choosing her words carefully now that she was getting Emily's cooperation. "Since you're *dressing* to go out with him, he apparently took the bait. Tell me how you trapped him."

"I didn't. Well, I tried to, but then I didn't have to."

"Come again?"

"Well, I was going to trick him into thinking that the treasure of Becket House really existed and keep him busy trying to track it down while I worked my charms on him. But then we found this letter in the fireplace and . . . well, it's kind of a long story, but we think it really does exist."

"Emily, have you had a checkup lately? I know of this truly wonderful holistic chiropractor who can cure any—"

"No. No. It's true," she insisted, and while she tried to get dressed and hold one ear and her mouth to the phone, she told Jennifer about their discovery.

"I don't believe this. You actually know where the gold is?" Jennifer asked in shock and amazement.

"Well, no. Not for true and certain. But we're going to dig around where we think it might be," Emily said, not wanting to get Jennifer's hopes up in case they were wrong or in case someone had come for the gold after Maggie's letter was written.

She was trying to zip up her dress, put her shoes on, and reassure her cousin when the front doorbell rang.

"He's here. I have to go. I love you. I'll call you tomorrow and let you know if we find anything," she said all at once, hanging up the phone before Jennifer could protest or ask another time-consuming question.

"I'm coming," she called from the top of the stairs. "I'm coming," she called again halfway down the stairs. "I'm here," she said, breathless as she opened the door.

"Yes, you are, and you're beautiful," Noble said, swooping through the doorway for a kiss as if it had been eons since the last time they'd enjoyed such sweet delights. "It was worth the wait."

"It wasn't all my fault," she said in her defense. She turned on the front porch light and closed the door behind her, saying, "Jennifer called."

"Oh. Let me guess. She wanted to know if we were sleeping together yet and if I was any good in bed. Right?"

"Well, yes. I'm pretty sure that's what she wanted to know. But she knew better than to just come right out and ask me. So, we were playing Twenty Questions, and she was going to draw her own conclusions."

"Women. And they say men talk." He was teasing her, and his high spirits were infectious. Not that Emily needed to be infected. She couldn't remember being happier or so lighthearted.

They decided to walk to the park in the town square, which was only eight blocks away. The night was cool enough to warrant her wearing a sweater, but warm enough to be a promise of the summer to come.

The elderly musicians were already there and setting up their instruments in the large belvedere commanding the center of the green when Emily arrived on Noble's arm.

"So. This is the young buck you've thrown me over for, Emily?" Bernie asked, surveying Noble with a critical eye.

"You must be Bernie. Emily talks about you all the time," the young buck said with a smile, receiving a cocky nod of the older man's head and a friendly slap on the shoulder for his trouble.

"Well, if that's all the two of you have to talk about, I'm surprised you're still keeping company," Gertie said, coming to stand next to Noble, batting her mascara-coated lashes at him. "There can't be anything less romantic than dull talk."

"She calling me dull?" Bernie asked Emily when it became apparent that he and she were suddenly excluded from the conversation. She shrugged and grinned and looked up at Noble in time to see him wink flirtatiously at Gertie.

"I couldn't agree more. I do my best, but you know how poor Emily is . . ." he said, trailing off hopelessly with a shake of his head.

That was the beginning of a night-long dalliance between Gertie the veteran vamp and the enamored young professor. While Emily and her troupe of players set up, the two of them sailed around the park, arm in arm, heads together, deep in discussion.

The band of volunteer boy scouts who'd been asked to set up chairs had done a fine job, and a crowd began to gather on the green. When the eight musicians started off with the lively tune "Won't You Come Home, Bill Bailey," Emily took a seat in the front row to lend support and was soon joined by Noble on her right and Gertie on his right.

The first set was entertaining, with songs ranging from "Can-Can Polka" to "Dixie." During the brief intermission the "stars" came off the platform to mingle with friends and loved ones in the crowd. It touched Emily deep inside to see them proudly strutting through the group, their heads high, their eyes lit up. To her, it was the way old age was meant to be.

"Well, I have to hand it to him," Gertie said, leaning over Noble to speak to Emily. "Ol' Bernie is holding his own right nicely, I think."

"They all are. I'm so proud, I could pop," she said. She glanced up at Noble and met the warm, adoring look that always caught at her heart and made it skip a few beats before it began to thump hard and heavy in her chest. "What do you think?" she asked him.

"I think you're terrific," he said in a low voice meant just for her. He bent his head and placed a quick, light seal of approval on her lips, and then in a more conversational tone he said, "They're great. I'm amazed at how much talent you found in such a small group."

The second set consisted mostly of old ballads. "Greensleeves" was Emily's favorite, and she couldn't help humming along. When they finally ran out of songs they all knew how to play, Chester Armstrong did a flashy rendition of "Oh, Susannah" on his banjo to close the show. All in all, with only a few notes out of key here and there, the evening was a great success.

"Come on, Grandma. We told Mom we'd be home by eleven," said Gertie's granddaughter as the crowd began to disperse. She was clad in black leather with an orange streak through her platinum-blond hair and seemed to have a great deal of patience and love for her grandmother.

Gertie gave the girl a disdainful look. "I swear, the worst day of my life was the day I failed the eye test for my driver's license and got thrown to the mercy of this . . . young person. Worst part about it is that she never breaks curfew."

"If I did, we'd both be without wheels. So, stop complaining and come on," the girl said, laughing.

By the time Gertie could be persuaded to leave Noble's side, almost everyone was gone. Only Bernie, his daughter, two of his young grandchildren, and Emily and Noble remained.

"I can't think of what's keeping my husband. He said he'd be here after the concert to pick up the electric keyboard and take it back to the center for us. If he doesn't come soon, the kids are going to fall asleep standing up. It's way past their bedtime," Bernie's daughter said, eagerly searching the streets for a familiar vehicle.

"Go ahead and take the kids home, honey. I'll wait for John, and he can drop me off on his way home," Bernie said, not liking to put his daughter to any extra trouble. He lived alone in a small apartment and was extremely independent. He hated having to ask someone, even his daughter, for help with anything.

"I have an even better idea," Noble said from his reclining position on the steps next to Emily. "Why don't you all go home. Emily and I can wait for your husband. We're on foot tonight anyway. A few minutes here or there isn't going to make any difference."

Father and daughter looked at each other, then back at Emily and Noble. "Are you sure you don't mind?" Bernie asked.

"Of course not," Emily answered, smiling at him fondly. "You put on a wonderful show tonight. Let us worry about the piano for a little while."

Alone in the park with Noble, the bright stars above pinned to a clear night sky and the air scented with springtime, Emily felt as if she were living one of those rare moments in life. Her heart was filled to the brim with expectation and happiness, contentment and joy.

Silent, they sat on the steps, communing with the universe. Emily sensed a oneness with the world, as if simply loving Noble put her in sync with everything around her. It was almost as if Noble had always been that tiny little missing piece of her that kept her out of step in the parade of life. Now that he was a part of her, she marched in unison—not awkwardly, not alone, and not as an outsider. Taking Noble into her heart connected her to infinity, because her love for him was something eternal.

"I'm getting really nervous, Emily. I've never seen you this quiet before." Noble's voice came from behind her. She turned and found him on the platform, plunking absently on the keyboard. He glanced in her direction, and although it was a quick gesture, she could see the concern in his expression. "Is anything wrong?"

"No," she said, standing up to join him. "I was just thinking how right my life seems tonight."

The smile he gave her was a gift of gentle understanding. "So, you're feeling it too. I thought maybe it was just me."

She shook her head slightly. "It isn't only you," she assured him, her whole body quickening at the sight of the passionate fires burning in his dark, fathomless eyes.

She knew what he wanted and didn't try to hide the fact that she wanted the same thing. They wanted to touch and be touched, join as one, and frolic in the exquisite delight of their love. But in a public park? They laughed together at the impossibility of it.

"I know that tune," she said, distracting herself with the melody Noble was playing over and over. "It's an old one. What is it?"

" 'Let me call you sweetheart, I'm in love with you,' " he said more than sang as he played the lilting tune. " 'Let me hear—' "

Suddenly the floodlights and electrical power in the belvedere went off, surprising them both. Emily laughed. "We only requested electricity until eleven-thirty," she said, looking around the park, now dark except for the low-glowing streetlights around the periphery. "I guess that's the end to the serenade," she said, disappointed.

With the speed of light, Noble had Emily in his arms. He waltzed her across the great round floor in the moonlight as he half spoke, half sang:

" 'Let me call you sweetheart, I'm in love with you.
Let me hear you whisper that you love me too.' "

She smiled and gave herself up to the playful romance of the moment, trying to pretend they were Fred and Ginger, knowing they looked more like Mickey and Minnie.

" 'Keep the lovelight glowing in your eyes so true,
Let me call you sweetheart, I'm in love with you.' "

He stepped off the platform and reached up for her. Effortlessly, without missing a word or a beat, he repeated the song and whirled her off into the shadows of the night.

"I'll be your sweetheart," she told him as they danced around the base of a huge oak tree. "But what about Gertie?" she asked, teasing him.

"Her eyes aren't as true as yours. They don't say they love me when they look at me the way yours do."

"Maybe that's because she doesn't love you the way I do."

Noble's mouth found hers in the darkness. The desire and longing she'd seen earlier in his eyes was there in his kiss as he pulled her close and possessively took what she offered. The soft, sensual, featherlike touching of their lips grew hard and devouring. Their tongues searched, teased, and mated. Their hands wandered, aroused, and found warm, yearning flesh. Hearts pounded, knees bent, and soon the impossible became a reality.

Emily tried to control the silly giggle in her throat as she searched on her hands and knees for her other shoe. She'd never felt more ridiculous—or less stressed about it.

"Which way did you throw my shirt, Emily? I can't see a damned thing out here," Noble complained as he explored in a like fashion in the opposite direction. He'd already apologized twice for not using more control, feeling overly guilty for the potentially embarrassing situation he'd gotten them into. "You won't think this is so funny when Bernie's son-in-law gets here and finds us naked in the bushes." He paused. "What *is* so damned funny over there?"

"It's gone," she said tightly, and then she couldn't hold it in any longer. She collapsed into a hysterical fit of laughter, rolling to the damp grass when her arms refused to support her. "It's gone," she wailed between gasps.

"What's gone?"

"The piano."

Ten

"What?" Emily muttered into her pillow, still trying to ignore Noble's elbow as he persistently nudged her awake.

"You have company," he said in a voice only slightly less drugged with sleep than her own. They'd made love and told intimate secrets well into the night, falling asleep when the sun dawned and exhaustion slurred their words.

"I know," she said, groaning lovingly, cuddling closer, wrapping an arm across his chest and giving him an affectionate squeeze.

"Not me. Downstairs at the front door." It was then she heard the doorbell for the first time. "Want me to see who it is?"

Emily didn't care if the whole world knew she was sleeping with Noble, but there didn't seem to be any point in flaunting it and creating a greater flurry of gossip than was necessary. She rolled out of bed and staggered out of the room, saying, "No. But if they don't leave right away, you can come down and shoot 'em."

"You got it," he muttered. She heard the sheets rustling as he turned over to go back to sleep.

A few minutes later she opened the front door and tried to focus sleepy eyes on the homely face of Amos Macky, chairman of the board of trustees for the college. Harder than trying to get a clear picture of his face was trying to come up with a logical reason for his presence at her front door on a Sunday morning.

"Emily, why didn't you call me. This is better than Al Capone's vault. We could have gotten national television coverage on this story. Geraldo would have jumped on this in a second," Amos said without so much as a good-morning-Emily. He was excited about something—and perturbed with her.

"Good morning, Amos. What are you talking about?"

A short dark-haired man in a poor-fitting gray suit rushed up behind Amos, asking, "You Emily Becket?"

"Yes." Her bewilderment increased a thousand-fold as she came fully awake. "Who . . ."

"Is it true that you've discovered gold in your backyard? Have you unearthed the treasure of Becket House after all this time? One hundred years, right? Was it really a federal payroll during the Civil War? Is it in coin or bullion or just paper money?"

Emily just stared at the little man as if he were speaking Greek. Her mouth fell open when another man and then another joined him on the front porch, pushing Amos aside to pummel her with questions.

"Who are you? What are you doing here?" she called out over the barrage of words. "What's happening?"

Suddenly she felt Noble's presence behind her. His hand on her shoulder felt like a life preserver in a sea of confusion.

"What's going on here?" he asked. His voice apparently carried more authority than Emily's, or maybe it was his size and his obvious strength that were more intimidating to the men as he stood shirtless at Emily's side. But for whatever reason, calm settled on the front porch.

"Jim Scott, *The Virginia Daily*. Are you Professor McEntire?" one reporter asked, his pad and pencil poised. When Noble nodded, the man asked, "Is it true that Ms. Becket called you in to help find the treasure of Becket House after she discovered an old letter hidden in the house?"

"Professor McEntire," another reporter called out before Noble could answer. "Greg Perry, *Richmond Report*. What do you plan to do with the gold? Could we get a couple shots of you and the lady holding some of it?"

"Professor . . ." another started as Emily's muddled senses glommed onto a familiar sound at the back of the house and she turned her attention in that direction.

"Emily? Emily, honey. Where are you?" Jennifer's excited voice called from the kitchen.

Emily left Noble at the front door and met her cousin halfway down the hall.

"Lord almighty. There are reporters all over the place. I had to drive all the way around and use the back gate," Jennifer said, dropping a suitcase and her purse on the floor and flopping down on the old deacon's bench that had stood against the same wall for decades. "I called only three or four. It's amazing the way they propagate."

"Jennifer!" Emily's cry of dismay caught her cousin off guard. She looked confused. "Why did you call any reporters at all? I told you we weren't sure if the gold was there or not."

"Well, if it is, we'll make the front page all over

the country. Emily, this is so exciting. I can't believe you don't want to share it with the whole world."

"What I don't want to do is look like a complete fool to the whole world if that hole out there is empty," she said, glancing over to see that Noble had stepped out onto the porch and looked as if he were directing traffic.

"He *does* look luscious without a shirt." Emily's head spun around to catch Jennifer with her thumbnail between her teeth, carefully assessing Noble's masculine form as if she had nothing better to do.

"Jennifer! For crying out loud. How are we going to get rid of these people?"

"I don't think we are," Noble said, closing the front door. He didn't look happy. In fact, from the look in his eyes, Emily got the impression he was very angry. But he remained calm and spoke with a level voice. "I told them we didn't have any news for them, but I don't think they believed me. So, then I told them they were welcome to hang around, but they'd have to do it down by the front gate."

Four eyes stared at Jennifer until she began to squirm in her seat. "Well, I thought it was a great idea. LOVERS FIND GOLD AT END OF RAINBOW," she titled her headline, waving her hand through the air dramatically.

Emily groaned and turned her face to the wall. Had it been just the night before when everything in her life had seemed so right? She began to hope this was all a very bad dream and that Noble would be kissing her awake very soon.

"I like the story angle," Noble said, humor creeping back into his voice. "But it's a little premature."

"You're not lovers yet?" Jennifer was aghast.

"We haven't found the gold yet," he told her patiently.

"But you will. Why else would old Maggie write the letter?"

Emily and Noble exchanged glances. Jennifer, frustrating as she was, had a point. And there was no other way to find out other than to go look.

Jennifer was left to make coffee while Emily and Noble went upstairs to get dressed.

"I'm sorry. I shouldn't have told her, I guess," she said once they were alone. "I had no idea she'd do something like this."

Noble laughed, obviously seeing something funny in the situation. He planted a quick kiss on her lips and said, "Don't worry about it, my sweetheart. It'll all come out in the wash. If it's not there, we'll just explain what happened and tell them it was taken away after the letter was written. And if it is there, you, me, and Jennifer will have our picture in all the papers."

"Captioned: LOVERS AND COUSIN FIND GOLD AT END OF RAINBOW," she added with a giggle, feeling a little better. She couldn't help but still feel a little resentful toward Jennifer, though—and toward herself for telling her. It had been hers and Noble's secret. She hadn't wanted to share the discovery with anyone but him. She shouldn't have boasted about the damned trap. It shouldn't have existed in the first place.

They took their time dressing and drinking coffee, hoping the reporters would get tired of waiting and leave. But they were a tenacious bunch that not only stayed but grew in number. They even spawned a mobile video crew from Washington, D.C.

The local police showed up. They parked both

cars down by the main gate, and at Emily's request promised to keep the reporters at bay until they were able to make a general announcement.

Noble tore the floorboards out of what remained of the gazebo as the press looked on from a distance. Jennifer, in her white linen pants suit, was of invaluable assistance as she took her turn carrying small pieces of wood gingerly to the woodpile and throwing them onto the heap. All the while Emily grew more and more anxious as she labored with the larger pieces of lumber and wondered what would be found at the bottom of the old well.

But she soon discovered that Noble, too, was itching to get to the answer of the one-hundred-year-old riddle. The opening in the floor of the platform barely exposed the well before he reached down and removed the planking that had covered the hole in the ground for so many years.

He looked over at Emily and grinned. His anticipation was contagious. She returned his smile, and he motioned her forward to join him above the shaft and to peer down into the darkness.

"It's bigger than I thought it was yesterday. I think I can go down without any trouble. But if it's shrunk to the point where we can't get the box out, we'll have to start digging," he said, his fingers inching over to cover hers. "Do you want to go with me?"

She looked back down at the hole. It was bigger than she remembered too. Hand-dug wells were a *lot* bigger—and deeper and darker—than she had pictured in her mind. Given the size of the pit and length of time it had been there, she suspected the unseen bugs lurking inside to be as big as her fist. "Ah. No. I think I'll skip it this time."

Her reluctance and the squeamish expression on her face made Noble chuckle. "Okay, chicken. I'll go alone, and you can stay up here and yell for help if I get stuck—or if something gnaws the rope in half," he said, using an eerie voice to tease her. When her frown deepened, he ruffled her loose mass of curls with his hand and laughed indulgently at her phobia. "Where's the flashlight?"

She watched Noble climb down off the platform and gather up the equipment he might need to get to the bottom of the well. He strapped a safety belt around his waist and buckled it securely between his legs before tying one end of a thick, coiled rope to it. He seemed so sure of what he was doing, as if he'd done it a hundred times before. So why was Emily suddenly having second thoughts?

Why did she feel the urge to throw the lid back over the top of the hole, walk away, and forget all about it? Why did she feel like Pandora all of a sudden? She shook her head in an effort to dispel her doubts. They were silly. What was the worst thing that could happen? Either the treasure was there and they'd end up famous, or it was gone, in which case Noble would have had his fun, his great-great-grandfather would be cleared of the charges, the legend would finally be put to rest, and they could all live happily ever after. What could possibly go wrong?

"Emily. How can you just sit there like that? Aren't you excited?" Jennifer asked, practically dancing with anticipation as she watched Noble prepare to lower himself into the hole. "I swear, i've never been this keyed up about anything before in my life. Emily. We're going to be rich."

"You're already rich," she reminded her cousin absently, disinclined to go into a lengthy discussion as to what the most likely fate of the treasure would be.

"You can't be too rich."

"So I've heard."

"What is it with you? What a party pooper."

"Sorry," she said with a negligible shrug. "I'm just a little nervous about Noble going down there."

They stood while he anchored the rope and sat down with his legs dangling in the mouth of the well, ready to start down into it.

"Tie that other rope to the back of my car the way I showed you yesterday and send the free end down to me," he told Emily. "When I call out to you, use the car to help pull the box up. Okay?"

She nodded. She took up the rope and turned to do as he asked. When he spoke her name softly, she looked back to see him curling his index finger at her.

"Don't I get a good-luck kiss? There could be huge mutant spiders and rats down there, you know."

"Noble!" Her one-word exclamation was full of horror and disgust and made him laugh merrily.

"Well, that's what you're thinking, isn't it? You have such a strange look on your face."

She bussed him quickly on the lips.

"Just go and get it over with," she said, making light of her trepidations. It would be too hard to explain the feeling she had. The feeling that whatever was about to happen was going to change their lives forever. She hadn't gotten used to her life being so perfect with Noble in it yet. She wasn't ready to have anything change so soon.

He leaned over to give her a real kiss, and murmured, "Don't worry," before he slid off the edge of the pit and descended into the darkness.

"Talk to me, Noble," she called when she couldn't

see him any longer, her voice echoing in the emptiness. "I want to be able to hear your voice."

"Ohhh . . ."

"Dammit, Noble."

His laughter was resounding.

"What's wrong?" Jennifer asked, coming up to stand beside Emily. Until now she'd been keeping her distance from the entrance of the well. But Emily's tone of voice lured her closer.

"Noble's being cute," she said, impatient. Then, turning back to the hole, she called, "How far down are you?"

"I don't know. But this isn't exactly as dry as I thought a dry well would be. The walls are getting soft and muddy."

Emily let several seconds of silence pass until she couldn't take it anymore, and hollered down into darkness once more. "Noble?"

"I'm still here. I think . . . awk. Oh, jeez."

"What?"

"I hit bottom, and it's covered with mud—halfway up my leg. Yuk."

"What about the gold?" Jennifer called.

"Hang on. I can't see as far as the end of my nose down here."

The stillness was excruciating. There was no sound to tell them if he'd gotten the flashlight out of his pocket, or if he was moving, or if he'd been smothered in the mud.

"Noble?" Emily could hear the panic in her own voice.

"Shhh," Jennifer hissed. "What's that noise? Is he whistling?"

They both held their breath. A faint trilling sound came from the bottom of the pit. Emily grinned as she recognized the tune. Oddly enough, it affected her more coming from the obscure depths of the well than it had in the moonlight the night before. Was there ever a sweeter, more loving man than Noble, she wondered with a sigh of contentment.

She felt each moment slip past her as they waited for Noble to speak again. Twice more he whistled the tune, faltering now and again as if he were distracted. But the tune would start again, and, impatiently, Emily would listen.

All at once it happened.

"Emily! It's here. I found it." She had no trouble imagining the expression on his face from the exuberance in his voice. She wanted to say something equally enthusiastic, but the words wouldn't form in her mind.

"How much gold is there?" Jennifer called, always ready with a response, even in—or perhaps especially in—a melodramatic moment. This quality of hers never ceased to amaze her cousin.

"I don't know. It's a wooden chest. It's covered with mud. I think we're going to have to do some digging to get it out. Can you round up another rope and a couple of buckets to haul the mud out with?"

Emily gave Jennifer strict instructions not to leave the well and to maintain constant contact with Noble while she ran to the house in search of buckets. For the next hour or more the two women lowered their containers down to Noble, who filled them with thick, clay-streaked mud. Jennifer became so caught up in the moment that she actually forgot to stay impeccably clean. The rich wet soil staining her linen suit went unnoticed as she pulled her share of the mud from the well.

"Send the ropes down empty next time," Noble instructed them from the darkness. "I think that ought to do it."

"Thank heaven," Jennifer said with a groan, dropping her bucket as she took in the state of her grubby disarray.

Emily, also muddied from head to toe, untied the buckets and sent the ropes back down to Noble. When she asked if he wanted the ropes tied to the back of his car again, he answered no. He planned to come up first and help pull the chest out of the well.

He emerged looking like Rambo in *First Blood Part II*. Noble had the stuff caked in his hair and all over his face and body. For the first time since the moment she'd set eyes on him, Emily didn't relish the idea of being held in his arms.

"You're a mess," she told him outright, grimacing.

"Look who's talking," he said, grinning, as he removed his mucky T-shirt. Then he shook his head regretfully, saying, "I guess we'll just have to take another shower when we're done here."

"Okay," agreed Jennifer, unaware that she hadn't been included in his invitation. "Then we'll go out and celebrate our discovery."

Noble and Emily exchanged glances and grins good-naturedly. They weren't about to let her intrude on their shower time, but they didn't really mind her assumption that the discovery of the treasure was now "theirs." It would always be their adventure. The gold would wind up back in government hands eventually, anyway, but no one, not even Jennifer, could take away the memory or the special bonding they'd shared.

Lost in Noble's rendition of a quick garden-hose shower, wondering how many times she'd have to make love to his perfect body before the mere sight of it ceased to arouse her, Emily was startled when pandemonium suddenly broke loose around them.

"Professor. Ms. Becket," called a reporter, advancing on them rapidly from the direction of the hedge wall that ran laterally along the property line, camcorder in tow. "Is the well empty, or have you found the treasure of Becket House?"

The reporters at the front gate saw him sprinting across the hundred yards that separated the hedge from the gazebo, and all at once a protest broke out. A steady stream of newspeople slipped past the two uniformed policemen and the gate, up the drive, and into the acreage behind the house.

They must have been sharing information and inventing new questions down at the gate as one query overlapped another. It soon became too difficult to even attempt coherent answers.

In the end it was Jennifer who tamed the inquisition by stepping forward in her bold, self-assured way and explaining clearly that something had been found at the bottom of the well, that they were welcome to stay and quietly watch the disinterment, and that all their questions would be answered one at a time once they knew what they had. This was apparently agreeable to all, as the reporters backed away to await the conclusion of the story, and Emily, Noble, and Jennifer returned to the well to finish their task.

Eager expectation and anticipation filled the silence as the three of them pulled heavily on the ropes. Emily was acutely aware of the warmth of the midday sun on her face and the smell of honeysuckle in the air. She had a detached feeling, as if she were watching instead of participating. She was excited, her senses finely tuned to her surroundings, but she couldn't believe she was actually digging up a lost treasure. It felt too unreal to her.

They refused offers from several of the reporters to help pull the box from its deep grave. By silent mutual consent they wanted to see it through to the end alone. And then, finally, one end of the old chest appeared in the opening of the well.

Noble inched forward and grabbed the ropes where they joined, using his beautifully sculptured muscles to haul the object onto solid ground. In the back of her mind Emily hoped someone had taken a picture of him. It would be a travesty to let such a beautiful display of the human form go unrecorded. She watched as he removed the ropes from the mud-encrusted box.

The leather-covered wooden chest had weathered the years well. The cowhide used to protect the contents of the box had certainly served its purpose. It was dark with age, moldy and cracked, but essentially intact. It was almost as if it had been fashioned to last forever—or until it was found.

There was no lock on the latch, but the metal had fused itself together due to oxidation. Noble used the crowbar from the trunk of his car to break the bond.

The three of them knelt beside the chest, impervious to the reporters. They exchanged ebullient glances and animated grins as they savored the moment. The feeling they shared was better than Christmas, better than a surprise party, not quite like a sexual thrill, but something very akin to it, and certainly it ranked high among their unforgettable moments.

Emily was so beside herself with excitement, she actually released a tiny squeak of uncontrollable elation as Noble slowly disengaged the lid.

Expecting to see gold coins or possibly bullion, it took several moments for her brain to register what she was actually seeing. Her heart grew sluggish, beating apathetically in her chest as the whole world grew dark and closed in around her. The chest was empty.

Vaguely she heard Jennifer's groan of dismay and sensed Noble's disappointment. But she turned totally into herself as she realized what the implications of the nondiscovery truly meant. She looked first at Noble, and then at Jennifer, knowing that the truth hadn't yet occurred to them. She grew numb waiting for it to hit them, until finally she could wait no longer.

"It was a lie," she uttered, the words sounding empty in her ears as both Noble and her cousin looked at her in confusion. "It was all a lie."

"What?" they asked almost simultaneously.

Then Noble added, "We knew it might not be here."

"No. We figured we'd either find the gold or there wouldn't be *anything* in the well," Emily said, angry because they weren't seeing things the way she was. "Don't you understand? It was all a lie. All of it. The legend. The man. All of it."

Their stupefied expressions were blurred as tears welled in her eyes. They didn't understand. And she couldn't bring herself to speak the words out loud. She'd always believed she could take pride in who she was and where she'd come from. Her heart withered with pain in the knowledge that William Joseph wasn't a war hero, wasn't an honorable man worthy of becoming a legend. He was nothing more than a common thief, a traitor to his cause, a criminal. He'd spent the money. He'd taken it and used it for his own purposes, and for generations Beckets had sung his praises, held their heads high, basked in the glory of his deeds, always assuming him to be a hardworking, honest man.

She looked at Noble, whose attention had been diverted by one of the reporters. He was answering the questions good-naturedly, as if nothing were amiss. Yes, they'd found a letter saying that the gold was placed in the well, but William Joseph had been waiting for Rebel troops to come and retrieve it, which is what obviously happened, he was saying, laughing at the outcome of their treasure hunt.

"If that's the case, Professor, can you hazard a guess as to why they didn't leave the gold in the box? Why would they take the gold and not the box?" a reporter wondered, innocently asking the fifty-million-dollar question.

Emily saw Noble's frown. She watched as he tried to calculate a logical answer. She died inside when he came to the only conclusion possible and lowered her eyes when he looked at her. Her shame kept her from meeting his gaze. She gagged on her pride and felt panic rise up within her as he searched her face for more answers.

Before all the ramifications occurred to him, before he could feel the disgust of knowing that his great-great-grandfather had died because of the greed of her own, Emily ran. She ran away from the well, away from Noble, and away from the truth. She couldn't face any of them, not ever again.

Eleven

Hunger and the call of nature finally impressed upon Emily that she was going to have to get out of bed eventually. She rolled over onto her stomach and looked out her bedroom window at the darkness that had gradually consumed the day's bright light. She was glad the day had come to an end and was already dreading the dawn of the next.

She tried to make her mind a total blank. She listened to the crickets and was grateful for the relative quiet. It had seemed like forever before the reporters had left. The rumbling of their questions and comments had lasted long after she'd fled and secluded herself in her room.

Noble's knock had come seconds after she'd thrown herself on her bed in a fit of despair.

"Emily?" he'd called, concern deepening his voice. "Emily? Can I come in?" He'd tried the door and found it locked. "At least talk to me."

"Go away, Noble."

"No."

"Yes. I want to be alone."

"Why? What's wrong? Why'd you run off like that?"

"You know why. He was a thief. A traitor." Tears fell, and her chest began to ache with pent-up sobs. "He was the cause of your great-great-grandfather's disgrace. He drove him insane and caused his death. I can't talk to you."

"That's stupid. Open the door and . . ." Emily had covered her head with her pillow to muffle his voice.

Either catatonia had set in or she'd fallen asleep, because next she heard Jennifer's voice calling to her.

"Emily, what is the matter with you? I took care of most of the reporters. The rest don't want to leave until they've talked to you. And frankly, I'm tired of making up excuses for you."

"I'm sorry, Jennifer. I just can't talk to them."

"Honey, what's wrong? Why are you acting like this?"

Emily couldn't believe that Jennifer hadn't realized yet where the money had gone or what it meant to their lives. She eased herself off the bed and opened the door a crack to peer out at her cousin. "Don't you understand what this means, Jennifer? William Joseph stole the money. He used it to build his estate. He grew rich and powerful on the blood of others. He built the college as a memorial to himself, and we've been basking in his tarnished glory ever since. He made fools of us all. I'm so ashamed, I can't look at myself in the mirror for fear I'll see a part of him in me."

"That's rubbish," Jennifer stated, a disgusted grimace on her face. "You don't have anything to be ashamed of. You didn't steal the gold."

"No. But I've participated in the crime. All my life I've boasted to people about what a fine, honorable man he was. I convinced people that the treasure of Becket House couldn't possibly exist because *my* great-great-grandfather was too honest a man not to see that it eventually got to the proper authorities, *if* he was involved in the story at all."

"So, you were wrong. It still doesn't have anything to do with who you are," Jennifer pointed out with remarkable logic.

"But it does. Don't you see? So much of me is the pride I've taken in coming from good, honest people. I was proud to be a Becket. Proud of the name. Proud to have been descended from a dirt-poor farmer who made the name honorable with his hard work and integrity. I knew who I was, and where and what I'd come from, and I was always able to hold my head up high. That's all changed now."

"Why don't I send Noble up to talk to you about all this? He's downstairs hiding in the kitchen, looking as if someone just ran over his dog," she said, hoping for a way out of the conversation.

"No. I don't want to talk to him. I can't face him. I don't think I'll ever be able to look him in the eye again." Tears spilled down her cheeks. "Please. Just tell him to go home. Home to Philadelphia. I don't want to see him ever again."

"Emily, you must be totally in love with Noble," Jennifer said as if realizing it for the first time, "or you wouldn't reject him over a silly little thing like bruised pride. Well, the situation is far more serious than I had suspected. Honey, do you have any Valium in there? Maybe a little more rest will help you see things more clearly," she said, feeling solicitous of poor Emily's dementia.

"Please. Please, just tell him to go. It's over for us."

She closed and locked her door again, and then crawled back onto the bed, ignoring the dried mud and dirt on the sheets. It seemed ironic to her that the crisp white linens she'd shared with Noble a few hours earlier should be stained and defiled with dirt from the past. Dirt touched by a thief and a traitor. Dirt she wouldn't have come anywhere near if she hadn't tried to trap and deceive Noble in the first place. Dirt she wouldn't have sullied herself with if she'd listened to her heart and been honest and truthful with him from the start.

The day faded away and grew quiet, almost too quiet. Her thoughts echoed loudly in the silence. She knew the reporters were gone, and she felt sure that Jennifer had given Noble her message and that he, too, was gone. If Jennifer hadn't left, she was showing incredible restraint in leaving Emily to herself, and she appreciated it.

But life, such as hers was at the moment, was going to have to go on. She knew the sun would come up in the morning, and she'd have to face the world and make the best of it. Ties with the college would have to be broken in order for it to survive once the truth was known to all. She seriously doubted that a college founded by Benedict Arnold would have fared well, and she wouldn't let Remount be associated with the Becket name. She gnawed on the possibility of having to deal with the federal government over the matter of the gold. Would they confiscate the house? Everything she owned? The possibilities were endless, and they weighed heavy in her heart.

Gathering her reserves, she sat on the edge of her bed, brushing small clumps of dried mud off the sheets. She couldn't remember the name of the president who'd told the world that the buck stopped with him, but she felt as if she ought to have it tattooed on her chest. She was the last Becket. She would pay whatever price was asked of her. She'd make amends to the world for her great-great-grandfather's sin and salvage the Becket name—not for him, but for her parents and their parents, whom she knew to be good people.

Fortified with these lofty thoughts, she gave into her hunger and her need to use the bathroom before her bladder burst. Imprisoning oneself in one's room could become very uncomfortable unless one had a connecting bathroom and a box of crackers—and some water. She was thirsty too.

A dim light shone in the upstairs hall from the floor below. The semidarkness and quiet lulled her into thinking she was alone and that she wouldn't have to confront anyone before she'd had time to gather up the rest of her defenses. By morning she'd have a clear plan of how to go about righting the wrong that had been done, she calculated as she hustled off to the bathroom, one door away.

Feeling fifty percent better after a quick shower, she wrapped herself in a clean terry robe, turned out the bathroom light, and started down the hall in search of some food. A Chinese dinner for four would just about satisfy the ache in her stomach, she decided, wondering at the resilience of human nature, glad she had her share of it.

"Hungry?"

"Ayah!" Noble's unexpected voice in the still, dark house scared the bageebees out of her. She swung around and staggered backward a little, grasping the banister for support. "Dammit, Noble, what are you doing here? You scared me to death."

"Good. Then that makes us even," he said, step-

ping out of the shadows so that she could see
him. His features were stony and not nearly as
handsome as usual. "I thought maybe you'd slit
your wrists in there. I was just getting ready to
kick the door in."

He didn't sound as if it made any difference to
him whether she slit her wrists or not. And that
made Emily mad. What the hell did *he* have to be
angry about?

"Where's Jennifer?" she asked.

"I asked her to go home. It seems you and I
have something to settle, and we don't need an
audience."

"I thought that's what I sent word for you to
do," she said, her ire rising to meet his as she
took an offensive stand in the middle of the dusky
hallway.

"I got the message. And Jennifer told me why
you sent it."

"So, then you understand why I don't want to
talk to you, why it would never work out for us
now."

"I don't understand any such thing," he bel-
lowed, his fury suddenly busting loose, out of
control. "I have never in my life heard of anything
so stupid. And where do you get off thinking you
can just call it quits between us without even
consulting me about it? Who the hell do you think
you are?"

Emily frowned. She'd never seen him angry before, never dreamed he could get so furious. Fear
was something she'd never felt in his presence
before. But she felt it now.

"I'm Emily Becket, and I can do anything I damn
well please," she told him, hands on her hips, feet
braced for a speedy retreat.

"Oh, yeah?" he said, stepping forward to put

his face near hers. "Well, I'm Noble McEntire, and I'm telling you that there's no way in hell you're going to get rid of me that easily. I want an explanation for all this nonsense, and it had better be damned good."

Emily judged the distance to her room and wondered if she could get in and have the door locked before he caught her. She didn't think so. He was standing so close to her, she could smell his heady aftershave and feel his breath on her face. She was glad she couldn't see his eyes too well. She was especially fond of his eyes and didn't relish the idea of seeing them when he was angry with her.

She didn't like his being angry with her at all, as a matter of fact. It hurt. It squeezed at her heart and made her stomach ache with a pain that had nothing to do with lack of nourishment.

Suddenly she wanted to touch him. She felt a need to reach out to him, to feel his arms around her. She hated this weakness in herself. She had wrongs to set right, and one of them was with Noble and his family.

"Don't you see, Noble, things are different between us now. What my great-great-grandfather did changes everything."

He backed off slightly, seeing that she was at least going to try to explain her feelings to him. But he was still infuriated, and he wasn't going to let her forget it. "No, I don't see it. Show me how it makes things different between you and me. Explain it to me."

"He was a thief. He stole from your great-great-grandfather, drove him insane, and caused him to commit suicide."

"And I'm supposed to blame you for that?"

"Well, even if you don't now, you would eventually. You have at least as much pride in your heritage as I used to have in mine. It would come between us, and you—"

"Hold it right there," he said, putting out a hand to stop her. "I'm beginning to get the picture. All this time we've been together, you've been thinking I was a thief because my great-great-grandfather was convicted of stealing and sent to prison and . . . and you've been thinking that I'm mentally unstable because he committed suicide. Is that right?"

"No. Of course not."

"Oh. Well, then you've been thinking that the only reason I've been hanging around is that you're a Becket and your family founded a college."

"No. I didn't think that." She shifted her weight from one leg to the other uneasily. He was accusing her of things that had never even occurred to her, and she didn't like it.

"Ah. So then you thought I was after the treasure of Becket House, and once I found it, I'd disappear."

"No! I didn't think any of those things. If I had, I wouldn't have—" She stopped herself mid-sentence, unwilling to confess her own dishonesty, to show the part of her that was so like old William Joseph. Lies and trickery seemed to be in her genes.

"You wouldn't have what?" he asked, watching her closely.

She straightened her shoulders and tipped her chin up defiantly. "I wouldn't have tricked you into coming here," she told him truthfully.

"You tricked me? How?"

"I baited a trap, and you fell for it," she said, not at all proud of her accomplishment.

"I did?"

"Yes, you did." When he didn't speak again, it

became apparent to her that he was waiting to hear how she had managed to trap him. She didn't debate telling him for long. She'd always believed in the truth, and the one time she hadn't been truthful, her life had shattered into a million pieces. She wanted to go back to being good ol' Emily, who always did her duty, could always be relied upon, and who always spoke the truth.

"I knew that what you were looking for wasn't in William Joseph's papers. I let you come to read them only so I could spend more time with you. I also knew about the vault in the fireplace. I . . . I didn't know about my great-great-grandmother's letter, though. That was a surprise to me too. But I did hide the page from William Joseph's papers in there for you to find."

"Why?"

"So you'd stay and look for a treasure that didn't exist. And so you'd feel better in at least being able to think that your own ancestor had been telling the truth all along."

"Even though you thought he was guilty."

She shrugged. She'd never really cared if the first Noble had stolen the gold or not. She'd tried to make him look innocent only because it meant something to his great-great-grandson.

"And it backfired on you," he concluded, and then he added thoughtfully, "You did all that just so I'd have to spend time with you."

She nodded, her chin almost touching her chest when she couldn't bring herself to meet his eyes. But the lights from below cut across the knuckles of his hands as he bunched them into tight, angry fists. He turned on his heel and took several paces down the darkened hall, using colorful cuss words to vent his anger. When he came back to her, his anger was barely controlled under his smooth, intimate voice.

"I don't think anyone has ever insulted me more than you just have, or disappointed me more. I don't know what I did to deserve it, and that sure as hell makes me mad. Because I don't think I do deserve it."

"You're right. You don't. I shouldn't have tricked you."

"Oh, I don't mind that. That's not why I'm mad. I think that's about the sweetest thing a woman's ever done for me."

Now Emily was confused. Her head came up, and she stood frowning at him in bewilderment. "Then why are you angry?"

"Because I was dumb enough to think you might be falling in love with me, that you trusted me. But I see I was wrong."

"You're not seeing it wrong. I do love you," she blurted out, suddenly desperate for him to know that truth as well.

"And did you love me when you thought my ancestor was an insane thief, or did you love me only after we discovered he was innocent?"

"I've always loved you. From the first time I saw you running past the front of the house, I loved you. I didn't even know who you were or where you'd come from."

"But you don't trust me enough to love you the same way. Isn't that what all this is about, Emily?" he asked, his voice hardly more than a soft whisper and harder than the cutting edge of a surgeon's scalpel. "Well, I gotta tell you, I do. The moment I saw you standing there in the hardware store, I knew you were the woman I'd always dreamed of. I recognized your face and knew you were the woman I'd love for the rest of my life. I didn't know who you were or where you'd come from either. It didn't matter then, and it doesn't matter now."

They stood face-to-face in the darkness, their breathing unsteady, their hearts hammering—one in excitement, the other in anger. Lord, how she wanted to touch him, to say she was sorry and to feel him close to her again. But she could still feel the fury surging through him and wasn't sure how he'd react. So, she remained silent, longing, waiting for the storm to pass.

It was Noble who broke the silence between them. "I'm leaving. I don't want you if you can't trust me, Emily." He brushed past her on his way to the stairs, and Emily thought she could actually feel his steps as they stomped across her heart.

"Noble, I . . ."

"No, Emily. I want more from you than just your love and your damned family tree. I'll be at home if you ever figure it out."

"Noble," she cried, but he was gone. She heard the slam of the front door and felt sick inside. Truth could sometimes set a spirit free—but in this instance it just plain hurt like hell.

Twelve

There was one good thing about big old houses that Emily hadn't considered before. When a person couldn't fall asleep in the middle of the night, there was plenty of room to roam around. By the time her journey took her to the kitchen, however, she found she couldn't stomach anything more than some weak tea and toast.

More heartsick than physically ill, she was listless and full of self-recrimination. The moment Noble had spoken the words, she'd known he was right. Absorbed in her self-pity, she hadn't given his feelings a second thought. She hadn't credited him with kindness, empathy, or even understanding. She hadn't believed that his feelings for her were anything more than superficial, which made him seem a very shallow man. She had wronged him terribly.

She ambled about on the first floor, straightening pictures, plumping pillows, and turning out lights until she was in total darkness at the bottom of the stairs. Exhausted in every sense of the word, she took the stairs slowly. Step by step.

What is pride, anyway, she wondered, trying to be objective. Self-esteem? Self-respect? The way you see yourself as a person. How *did* she see herself now that she knew William Joseph was a thief? Was she herself any less honest? Any less kind? Any less the person she had been yesterday? She hoped not. She'd liked that Emily.

That Emily knew who she was, what she wanted, and where she wanted to go. Did she still know all those things? She searched for a minute and then decided she did. She was still the same Emily. And Noble was the same Noble. Nothing had changed them because of what had been discovered in the well.

So, why had the change in the legend affected her so? Was it because of another kind of pride, she wondered. A conceited, artificial sort of pride that she'd used to make herself seem better than everyone else. Not a lot better, just a little bit better so that her life wouldn't seem so ordinary.

Instead of going into her room and on to bed when she reached the top of the stairs, she allowed her feet to carry her up the attic steps to where the whole mess had started.

Was her life ordinary? Yes. The answer was undeniable. She was an ordinary woman who lived in an ordinary town, who had an ordinary job. Was being ordinary so bad? She sighed a heavy sigh of relief when she finally made up her mind. No. Being an ordinary person wasn't bad at all.

The legend of old William Joseph had nothing to do with the reasons she'd come to live in Remount. She was happy in quiet places, she felt secure having people she knew and loved around her. It hadn't had anything to do with her choice of careers either. She had an innate understanding and respect for elderly people. She enjoyed their stories. She was amazed by their wisdom. And she just plain enjoyed their company.

Her father had taught her about honor and duty. Her mother had showered her with love and gentleness. She had accrued her own knowledge and opinions. These were the things in her life she should have been proud of.

She approached the desk and looked down at the metal box that contained William Joseph's papers.

"Damn stupid stuff," she cried, shoving the heavy box off the desk in one angry motion. "Why the hell didn't somebody throw you away years ago?"

Staring down at the papers scattered on the floor, the answer came to her. Slowly and in pieces the puzzle came together.

"Oh, dear Lord," she whispered. "It was here all the time."

She went down on her knees and began to take a close, hard look at the records that had been kept so carefully and passed down from one generation of Beckets to the next as if they'd been . . . gold.

This time her tears came from relief. She knew who and what she was. And she was happy to be just that. But old habits were hard to kill. She couldn't help being glad that the stories she'd grown up with and the things she'd believed to be true about the people who came before her were, in reality, true.

Every entry on the pages took on new meaning as she realized what they were. They were William Joseph's accounting of every penny he'd taken from the well. Every apple he'd picked, every pound of pig he'd sold was clearly documented. He'd taken the gold, invested it, and amassed a fortune. And for what? Well, that was recorded as well. Near the end he had used the greater part of the wealth to build the college. More went into the endowments and scholarships. What little that was left was either his to begin with or what he kept for a job well done, like his wages for a lifetime of hard work.

And why? Why had he spent his entire life laboring under the burdens of suspicion and fear of being caught with the gold? Maggie's letter came to mind. He'd promised that the gold would never fall into enemy hands, and he'd kept that promise throughout the war. After the war he'd have been in deep trouble if he'd tried to give it back, so he kept his second promise to Lieutenant Wakeland. He saw to it that it was used for the good of the South, for the lieutenant's favorite cause, education.

So it was over. The treasure was gone. The mystery was solved. Emily could still be proud of her ancestors and know that she came from honest, decent people—even though she knew they didn't have anything to do with who *she* was.

She gathered up the papers one more time with more reverence than she'd ever had for them before. She'd pass them on to her own children along with the true story someday, she thought pleasantly. She'd teach them to be proud of themselves not because of who they'd come from but because of who they were and what there was inside of them.

But first she had to figure out a way of getting those children. She glanced at the window and saw that dawn was breaking, and she smiled her first smile of the new day as her thoughts turned to Noble.

The door to Noble's rented room came open quickly in response to Emily's knock. He'd been waiting for her, but his mood didn't seem to have changed. He was still wearing his angry scowl. His stance and disposition were impatient. But those weren't the first things she noticed about him.

He was bare except for running shoes and shorts, which was always a thrill for her to behold. His hair was rumpled, and he hadn't shaved yet. He might have been sleeping, but he didn't look rested. In fact, he looked worse than she'd felt an hour earlier.

"Are you still angry with me?" she asked, hesitant. She didn't know where or how to start. She just wanted him to hold her.

"No," he said, the tone of his voice making it clear that he wasn't exactly happy with her either. "Every time I've thought about going back and wringing your neck, I've gone out for a run to cool off." He paused before adding, "I'm pretty sure that my landlady thinks I'm on drugs."

Emily smiled at his attempt to lighten the situation. It told her that he was indeed over his anger but still feeling the pain.

"May I come in?"

He nodded, watching her with a masked expression as he closed the door behind her and stood waiting to hear what she had to say.

They looked at each other for several seconds, making a short last-minute evaluation to see if risking an apology and granting forgiveness would be worth the effort in the long run. It was in those brief seconds that Emily felt a feeling of peace and an assurance that the outcome of this day had long ago been agreed upon by a force far more powerful and wise than the two of them.

Asking Noble's forgiveness was a mere formality. It was a symbol of respect, a sign of understanding, and a cleansing act of contrition, but a simple formality nonetheless. Because he'd already forgiven her, and she knew it. Noble loved her, and she knew that too. He knew her and understood her, because they were so much alike. And like Emily, he could forgive anyone anything if he loved them.

"I've come here to give you the apology I owe you. I treated you badly, and I'm sorry," she said, bold and sincere.

"And . . ." he prompted her, throwing a leg over one end of a low chest of drawers and crossing his arms across his chest.

"And?" she asked, bewildered. What else was there? Hadn't he ever seen the movie *Love Story?* She shouldn't have had to say she was sorry, but she'd wanted to because she'd hurt him. What was he asking for now, blood?

"And I want to know what kind of conclusions you came to about us," he said, his voice taking on a stronger tone.

"Well, actually, I came to only one conclusion."

"What was that?"

"That you and I have a lot more to offer each other than our family trees."

"Like what?" he asked. Nothing in his manner had changed, but Emily caught a look in his eyes that she had come to know very well. It was the smoldering glint he got when he touched her, before he kissed her, and always after they'd made love. It was a signal to her, a forewarning of the stormy passion building up within him. It was a look she loved and looked forward to.

"Do you want to hear what I think you have to offer me, or what I'm here to offer you?" she asked, fighting to keep a straight face now that she knew she was back in his good graces.

"Let's hear what you have to offer me." He leaned back against the wall as if he were a king holding court, waiting to accept or reject her best offers.

"I have almost two thousand dollars in my savings account."

That shook him. He sat up straight with a shocked expression and indignantly told her, "I don't want your money."

"Oh." She tried to appear disappointed. "Well, I own a very old house. It's in need of some repair, but it *is* a historical landmark."

He studied her thoughtfully for a moment and then stood up with his hands on his hips and a small defeated smile playing on his lips. "I don't want your house either."

"Oh, dear." She sounded a little like Nell talking to Snidely Whiplash. "My car's a piece of junk. It isn't worth anything. And if you don't want my money or the title to my home . . . well, then . . ." She took two steps closer to him. "All I have left to offer you . . . is me."

"That's all I ever wanted," Noble said, grinning. He closed the distance between them and scooped her into his arms, then he set her back on the floor and gave her a gentle kiss.

They passed a considerable time in that fashion before they spoke again.

"I really am sorry, Noble."

"I know. And I understand what a shock you've had, but I don't think it's nearly as bad as you were thinking. In fact," he said with a start and a snap of his fingers, "wait here. I'll be right back. I want to see if the morning paper has come yet."

He was out the door before she could stop him. She didn't want to see what the newspapers had to say about her great-great-grandfather. It would all be lies, because she was the only one who knew the real truth about him.

Resigned to the fact that she was going to have to get used to the idea of people thinking the worst about her family and that she was going to have to be satisfied to know in her heart that they were good, decent people, she sat down on the edge of Noble's bed to wait for him.

Bouncing just a little and swinging one leg back and forth absently, she reflected on the changes in her life over the recent weeks and smiled. She'd had the life she'd wanted before, but now she had everything she'd ever dreamed of. She had been content, but now she had great expectations as well. She had so much to look forward to, so much more to live for. And all because Noble had finally come into her life.

Noble, whose body was a source of perpetual excitement to her, whose charm had won her emotions. Wasn't it strange the way two people could suit each other so well, she pondered happily.

There was a plunk on the window, and she got up to look down into the street below.

"Too early," Noble called up through the open window. "I'm going to run down to the corner and get one. Make yourself at home. I'll be right back."

With a smile only a woman in love could produce, she watched him jog down the street and out of sight.

"Lord, that man's body just never quits," she said aloud, rolling her eyes heavenward. Automatically her gaze went to his bed. "Make myself at home, huh?"

She was suddenly very tired. If she were at home, she would call in sick at work and go to bed for the rest of the day, she figured, a cunning smile on her lips.

Emily could tell by her assistant's voice that she was a little surprised at the call. It was to be expected, she supposed, as she was rarely sick. But everyone was a little under the weather once in a while, right? Well, she planned to be under the bright, sunny, beautiful spring weather all day long—with Noble.

Naked, she crawled into his bed and got comfortable. She sighed happily and looked out the window at the clear blue sky that stretched out past infinity, just like her future.

The bed sagged and cool skin touched hers under the sheets. She'd dozed off and hadn't heard Noble come back. She came awake instantly, and looked up into his smiling face.

"I like the way you make yourself at home," he said, planting a light kiss on her lips.

"I thought you would." She reached out and wrapped her arms around his neck, cuddling closer.

"Don't you want to see what the papers have to say about our great discovery?" he asked even though that special lovelight was shining in his eyes.

"Not especially." She tried to nibble on his lower lip, but he moved away.

"It's really not so bad, Emily. I think you should read it," he said, producing the paper and holding it up in front of her nose.

The whole top half of the front page was a picture of her, Noble, and Jennifer kneeling beside the chest, moments before they opened it and discovered the truth. The looks of excitement on their faces were plain to see. If the photographer had waited a second or two longer, he could have gotten an even clearer shot of their shock and disappointment.

"Read," Noble insisted, obviously deciding that she'd pondered the picture and her memories of the previous day long enough.

She flipped the paper over and started to read. It was a fairly accurate account of what had happened, and there was even . . .

"Maggie's letter," she exclaimed, looking up at Noble for an explanation.

"Jennifer went down to the post office and had copies made for all the reporters. It tells the most accurate story of how we discovered where to look for the gold."

"Good idea. It makes him sound less like a cold-blooded thief," she said, thinking aloud.

"Well, skip that part and read down here, where they talked to me. I give one hell of an interview," he said, grinning.

"That's because you're so humble."

She scanned the page for his name and found it, but only after he'd impatiently tapped the opening paragraph several times with his index finger. "Read it out loud," he said.

She laughed at his excitement, and then began to read.

" 'Professor Noble McEntire, close friend to Ms. Becket and one of the principal treasure hunters—' " She stopped and looked up at Noble. "Is that what you are? My close friend?"

"Friends don't get any closer than lovers, and it was the best I could come up with, since you aren't my wife yet."

"Yet?"

"Yet," he repeated decisively. He kissed the tip of her nose, and then ordered her to read on.

"Well, I hope you're planning to get down on one knee and ask me. When I marry you I want—"

"Read."

"Okay. Blah, blah, blah . . . okay. 'When asked what he thought had happened to the gold, Professor McEntire stated: "I think it was used to build Remount College. There are fifty or sixty years' worth of documented records in the attic of Becket House that show how William Becket spent every nickel of it. He invested it in land and livestock, increasing the original amount until he had enough to do something worthwhile for the South with it." ' "

Emily looked up at Noble, flabbergasted. "How did you know?"

"Well, why else would anyone want to keep all that junk? Somewhere, sometime, they would have had to have been important to someone. And since it was very important to Maggie that William Joseph's name be kept clean, I figured she was the one who'd set them aside for future generations."

"You amaze me." Emily didn't even try to hide the awe in her voice.

"That's nothing. Wait till you get to the good part. Then you'll really see me in action and know what a great lawyer I am," he said, very cocky. "It's all in the summation."

" ' "It is my opinion," Mr. McEntire stated yesterday, "that William Joseph Becket was a decent, honorable man who remained a Confederate soldier long after the war was over, carrying out his final order from his commanding officer until the day he died." ' "

"Oh. That is chilling," Emily told Noble, dramatically showing him the impression it had made on her. She would have swallowed hot coals before she told him that she had come to the same conclusion just a few hours earlier. It meant so much more to her that it had been the first thing that had occurred to Noble and not the last. "I'm terribly impressed—and very grateful."

Noble just smiled, pleased because she was. Then his smile widened into a grin, and he said, "Ah, shucks, ma'am. That's nothing. If it's chills and thrills you want—which you obviously do because when I left here you had all your clothes on—I do a completely different act for that."

"You do?" Noble blindly eased the paper out of her fingers while he nuzzled her neck and sent those thrills and chills he'd promised racing up and down her spine. Emily giggled. With Noble in her arms, she had a feeling that no one would ever refer to her as "poor Emily" again.

THE EDITOR'S CORNER

We've selected six LOVESWEPTs for next month that we feel sure will add to your joy and excitement as you rush into the holiday season.

The marvelously witty Billie Green leads off next month with a real sizzler, **BAD FOR EACH OTHER,** LOVESWEPT #372. Just picture yourself as lovely auburn-haired journalist Keely Durant. And imagine that your boss assigns you to interview an unbelievably attractive actor-musician, a man who makes millions of women swoon, Dylan Tate. Sounds fascinating, doesn't it? So why would the news of this assignment leave Keely on the verge of a collapse? Because five years before she and Dylan had been madly, wildly attracted to each other and had shared a white-hot love affair. Now, at their first reunion, the embers of passion glow and are quickly fanned to blazing flames, fed by sweet longing. But the haunting question remains: Is this glorious couple doomed to relive their past?

Please give a big and rousing welcome to brand-new author Joyce Anglin and her first LOVESWEPT #373, **FEELING THE FLAME**—a romance that delivers all its title promises! Joyce's hero, Mr. Tall, Dark, and Mysterious, was as charming to gorgeous Jordan Donner as he was thrilling to look at. He was also humorous. He was also supremely sexy. And, as it turned out, his name was Nicholas Estevis, and he was Jordan's new boss. Initially, she could manage to ignore his attractiveness, while vowing never to mix business with pleasure. But soon Nick shattered her defenses, claiming her body and soul. Passionate and apparently caring as he was, Jordan still suspected that love was a word only she used about their relationship. Would she ever hear him say the cherished word to her?

Sandra Chastain, that lovely lady from the land of moonlight and magnolias, seems to live and breathe
(continued)

romance. Next, in LOVESWEPT #374, **PENT-HOUSE SUITE,** Sandra is at her romantic Southern best creating two memorable lovers. At first they seem to be worlds apart in temperament. Kate Weston is a feisty gal who has vowed to fill her life with adventure upon adventure and never to stay put in one place for long. Max Sorrenson, a hunk with a bad-boy grin, has built a world for himself that is more safe than thrilling. When Kate and Max fall in love despite themselves, they make fireworks . . . while discovering that building a bridge to link their lives may be the greatest fun of all.

If ever there was a title that made me want to beg, borrow, or steal a book, it's Patt Bucheister's **ONCE BURNED, TWICE AS HOT,** LOVESWEPT #375. Rhys Jones, a good-looking, smooth operator, comes to exotic Hawaii in search of a mysterious woman. At first he doesn't guess that the strawberry blonde he bumped into is more than temptation in the flesh. She is part of what has brought him all the way from London. But more, the exquisite blonde is Lani . . . and she is as swept away by Rhys as he is by her. She soon learns that Rhys is everything she ever wanted, but will he threaten her happiness by forcing her to leave the world she loves?

Welcome back the handsome hunk who has been the subject of so many of your letters—*Kyle Surprise.* Here he comes in Deborah Smith's **SARA'S SURPRISE,** LOVESWEPT #376. Dr. Sara Scarborough saw that Kyle had gotten through the sophisticated security system that guarded her privacy. And she saw, of course, the terrible scars that he had brought back from their hellish imprisonment in Surador. Sara, too, had brought back wounds, the sort that stay buried inside the heart and mind. Demanding, determined, Kyle is soon close to Sara once more, close as they'd been in

(continued)

the prison. Yet now she has a "surprise" that could leave him breathless . . . just as breathless as the searing, elemental passion they share.

From first meeting—oops, make that impact—the lovers are charmed and charming in Judy Gill's thrilling **GOLDEN SWAN,** LOVESWEPT #377. Heroine B. J. Gray is one lady who is dynamite. Hero Cal Mixall is virile, dashing, and impossibly attracted to B.J. But suddenly, after reacting wildly to Cal's potent kisses, she realizes this is the man she's hated since she was a teenager and he'd laughed at her. Still, B.J. craves the sweet heat of him, even as she fears he'll remember the secret of her past. And Cal fears he has a job that is too tall an order: To convince B.J. to see herself as he sees her, as an alluring beauty. An unforgettable love story!

Do turn the page and enjoy our new feature that accompanies the Editor's Corner, our Fan of the Month. We think you'll enjoy getting acquainted with Patti Herwick.

As always at this season, we send you the same wishes. May your New Year be filled with all the best things in life—the company of good friends and family, peace and prosperity, and, of course, love. Warm wishes from all of us at LOVESWEPT.

Sincerely,

Carolyn Nichols

Carolyn Nichols
Editor
LOVESWEPT
Bantam Books
666 Fifth Avenue
New York, NY 10103

FAN OF THE MONTH

Patti Herwick

I first heard of LOVESWEPTs in a letter from Kay Hooper. We had been corresponding for some time when Kay told me she was going to start writing for Bantam LOVESWEPT. Naturally, since Kay was special—and still is—I was eager for the LOVESWEPTs to be published. I was hooked from then on. I read books for enjoyment. When a book comes complete with humor *and* a good story, I will buy it every time. As far as I'm concerned, LOVESWEPTs haven't ever changed. The outstanding authors that LOVESWEPT has under contract keep giving us readers better and more interesting stories. I am enchanted with the fantasy stories that Iris Johansen writes, the wonderful, happy stories that Joan Elliott Pickart writes, and, of course, Kay Hooper's. I can't say enough about Kay's work. She is a genius, her writing has gotten better and better. Every one of her books leaves me breathless. Sandra Brown is my favorite when it comes to sensual books, and I enjoy Fayrene Preston's books also. The fact that LOVESWEPTs are so innovative—with books like the Delaney series and Cherokee series—is another reason I enjoy reading LOVESWEPTs. I *like* different stories.

Now, as for me, I'm 44 years old, married, and have one grandchild. I think that I've been reading since the cradle! I like historical romances along with the LOVESWEPTs, and I probably read between 30 and 40 books a month. I became the proud owner of my own bookstore mostly because my husband said if I didn't do *something* about all my books, we were going to have to quit renting our upstairs apartment and let the books take over completely! I enjoy meeting other people who like to read, and I encourage my customers to talk about their likes and dislikes in the books. I never go *anywhere* without a book, and this has caused some problems. One time, while floating and reading happily on a swim mat in the water, I floated away. My husband got worried, searched, and when he found me and brought me back, he decided to do something so he wouldn't have the same problem again. Now he puts a soft nylon rope around the inflatable raft and *ties* it to the dock! I can only float 50 feet in any direction, but I can read to my heart's content.

I would like to thank LOVESWEPT for this wonderful honor. To have been asked to be a Fan of the Month is a memory I will treasure forever.

60 Minutes to a Better, More Beautiful You!

Now it's easier than ever to awaken your sensuality, stay slim forever—even make yourself irresistible. With Bantam's bestselling subliminal audio tapes, you're only 60 minutes away from a better, more beautiful you!

__ 45004-2	**Slim Forever**	$8.95
__ 45112-X	**Awaken Your Sensuality**	$7.95
__ 45081-6	**You're Irresistible**	$7.95
__ 45035-2	**Stop Smoking Forever**	$8.95
__ 45130-8	**Develop Your Intuition**	$7.95
__ 45022-0	**Positively Change Your Life**	$8.95
__ 45154-5	**Get What You Want**	$7.95
__ 45041-7	**Stress Free Forever**	$7.95
__ 45106-5	**Get a Good Night's Sleep**	$7.95
__ 45094-8	**Improve Your Concentration**	$7.95
__ 45172-3	**Develop A Perfect Memory**	$8.95

NEW!

Handsome Book Covers Specially Designed To Fit Loveswept Books

Our new French Calf Vinyl book covers come in a set of three great colors— royal blue, scarlet red and kachina green.

Each 7" × 9½" book cover has two deep vertical pockets, a handy sewn-in bookmark, and is soil and scratch resistant.

To order your set, use the form below.

THE DELANEY DYNASTY

Men and women whose loves an passions are so glorious it takes many great romance novels by three bestselling authors to tell their tempestuous stories.

THE SHAMROCK TRINITY

☐	21975	**RAFE, THE MAVERICK** *by Kay Hooper*	$2.95
☐	21976	**YORK, THE RENEGADE** *by Iris Johansen*	$2.95
☐	21977	**BURKE, THE KINGPIN** *by Fayrene Preston*	$2.95

THE DELANEYS OF KILLAROO

☐	21872	**ADELAIDE, THE ENCHANTRESS** *by Kay Hooper*	$2.75
☐	21873	**MATILDA, THE ADVENTURESS** *by Iris Johansen*	$2.75
☐	21874	**SYDNEY, THE TEMPTRESS** *by Fayrene Preston*	$2.75

THE DELANEYS: *The Untamed Years*

☐	21899	**GOLDEN FLAMES** *by Kay Hooper*	$3.50
☐	21898	**WILD SILVER** *by Iris Johansen*	$3.50
☐	21897	**COPPER FIRE** *by Fayrene Preston*	$3.50

Buy them at your local bookstore or use this page to order.

Bantam Books, Dept. SW7, 414 East Golf Road, Des Plaines, IL 60016

Please send me the items I have checked above. I am enclosing $_____
(please add $2.00 to cover postage and handling). Send check or money
order, no cash or C.O.D.s please.

Mr/Ms _____

Address _____

City/State _____ Zip _____

SW7–11/89

Please allow four to six weeks for delivery.
Prices and availability subject to change without notice.

Special Offer
Buy a Bantam Book
for only 50¢.

Now you can have Bantam's catalog filled with hundreds of titles plus take advantage of our unique and exciting bonus book offer. A special offer which gives you the opportunity to purchase a Bantam book for only 50¢. Here's how!

By ordering any five books at the regular price per order, you can also choose any other single book listed (up to a $5.95 value) for just 50¢. Some restrictions do apply, but for further details why not send for Bantam's catalog of titles today!

Just send us your name and address and we will send you a catalog!